A Practical Potions Mystery

Practical Potions
and
Paranormal Proclivities

Wren Jones

To those who feel invisible.

May you feel seen in these pages
and find your voice by the end.

Content Warning

This book is a cozy mystery and there are many moments of slow decompression.

There is no on-page death.

However, it explores feelings of grief and loss. While this may feel heavy at times, the focus is always on healing.

If this isn't the right time for these themes -- it's okay.

You can always come back another time.

I write these books so you can feel like you opened the door to your cozy dream coffee shop where your friends are already sitting together, waiting for you with warm smiles.

With that in mind, the timelines between books are linear with character growth in each. But just the same way you can always skip a coffee date and pick up with your best friends like no time passed, these books are the same.

ONE

Beejee's Special

"WELL, at least you're awfully happy," Lohrna said. Her hands gripped the bow of the ship as though she was terrified if she loosened her hold she would tumble overboard. She was staring at Beejee, the tabby cat, with narrowed eyes as the ship bobbed up and down in the ocean waves gently.

Beejee's ear flicked but he kept his gaze to the horizon. "And you're not," he said. "Finally."

Lohrna gulped, then lowered her forehead to rest between her hands.

"Will you let me make you a brew of Beejee's Special Blend?" Sella asked her friend. She rubbed between Lohrna's shoulder blades gingerly. "I promise it won't give you spots."

Lohrna twisted her head and opened one eye to look up at Sella, her expression soured. "I didn't mind the spots," she grumbled. "Or the stink bomb…"

Sella smiled, remembering all their spells gone wrong

back when they were kids. Beejee had called Lohrna cursed. And it was true that whenever she was around, things did tend to go astray.

Though Sella knew then and now that it was her own ineptness that caused it. For now, she kept rubbing her friend's back gently and smiled through her friend's harsh stare. "Then, what do you mind?" Sella asked at last.

"I want to prove that I can do this," Lohrna said. "On my own."

"While the witch rubs your back, huh?" Beejee scoffed.

Sella rolled her eyes. She ignored Beejee. "You *can* do this, Lohr," she said. "But there's no sense in suffering. It's been days on board and you haven't found your sea legs. Just take the blend to stop the nausea, at least."

"Tell her I agree," Cali said, appearing just beside Sella with a little shimmer in her wake as she moved closer. "But either way, her suffering is coming to an end. We seem to be approaching." The ghost pointed to the front of the ship where a glimpse of land at the edge of the sea began to slowly appear.

Sella followed Cali's finger, her eyes squinting to where the bright, sparkling sea met the teal sky. She tapped Lohrna's back, a little stronger. "Cali says we're almost there," she said, nodding to the little speck of land.

Lohrna's head rolled to the side. "Thanks, Cali."

Calisyali, though a ghost only witches and familiars could see, had built a surprisingly close friendship with Lohrna over the years she had been dead. Somehow, through sheer force of will on both their parts, they had made it work. Cali was beaming now, a huge smile on her face, though a crease appeared between her brows.

Sella's eyes flicked to the approaching shore, then back to catch Cali's gaze just as her expression shifted.

"It will be strange… going back," Cali said, her voice so soft it carried away in the breeze like smoke.

Sella looked down at the waves below them, one hand still firmly on Lohrna's back.

Cali had a way of doing that. Of saying something that demanded a bigger conversation when they were in a crowded space. Of dropping something heavy when Sella couldn't really help.

Sella's eyes squinted into the deep blue waves and part of her wished she could stop the sea from bringing them any closer. She wanted to stop time and movement and just… be. But a bright, silver, blurry thing caught her eye. It was swimming alongside the ship, keeping a surprising pace, though it darted down into the depths anytime Sella's eyes landed on it for long.

She sighed, at last removing her hand from Lohrna and focusing on Cali. "Are you nervous?" she asked, loud enough for Lohrna and Beejee to hear. She was asking the group as much as the ghost herself.

It had been two years since Cali had landed on the shores of Orakan and tried to settle in as one of the few humans in a strange, rainy land. Two years since she was murdered in their small town for a Witch's Mark she didn't deserve. She rarely spoke of her family back home in the land of humans. And no one but a selfish ex-boyfriend had ever showed up to look for her in Marra after she died.

It all felt like a lifetime ago now.

All Sella really knew about her past was that her given name was Calisyali. Though as long as she had known her, she went by Cali since it was easier to say. She knew that her family were all military wyvern riders. That she left because she preferred a peaceful life working with numbers. And that when pressed on the matter, she shut down.

Sella had never been across the ocean. She had always admired Cali's bravery for making the journey on her own and arriving in a strange land filled with magic and strange creatures with an ever present smile on her face and willingness to help anyone.

Beejee's ear flicked. "The only thing I'm nervous about is helping Sediri with her potion shop. I still don't think she has earned our help."

"She won't be there much," Sella said. "She and her partner are traveling, I think. We're to help set things up and get it running while she's away."

"So we have to do even *more* work?" Beejee yowled.

"That's why I didn't tell you," Sella grumbled with a small shrug.

Beejee's eyes narrowed.

"I see land!" Cali cried, breaking their standoff. It was loud enough that Lohrna's ear twitched beneath her cascades of black curls.

Lohrna lifted her body a bit and squinted into the distance. "Oh, thank the tides. Land…"

TWO

Dessert in the Desert

SELLA KNEW that Tollintal would be different. Over the years, she listened eagerly to Cali talk about her former home. A strange place where the plants grew low to the ground, never reaching the height of the tall trees they had in Marra. The ghost told her that most of them were adorned with needle-like spikes instead of lush leaves. And that as a child she had fallen into a big batch of them trying to retrieve a toy that had been thrown in the middle.

It was a place where the ground got so dry that it cracked open, spiderwebbing like broken glass in the summertime as the water grew scarce. A place where the sky was always bright blue in the daytime and people liked to gather to watch it transform to bright orange and pink when the hot sun rose and set.

It had always been a dream of Beejee's to travel across the sea and her stories only fueled his fascination. Because for all its peculiarity and sometimes unnerving descriptions, it also sounded beautiful both in nature and in culture. In the land of humans and a place with a long history of conflict, shifters and witches were, somewhat ironically, more accepted than in Orakan. Cali had told them that here, witches were abundant, and allowed to practice whatever kind of magic they wanted to.

Sella had wondered what it would be like for Lohnra to be among others like her. A place where shifters were not asked to hide themselves. Lohnra had made friends with the Mild and Mannerly Brotherhood of Shifters, Sisters Accepted group that had blown into town with a festival the year before. Slowly, she was learning to find her own path to acceptance as she didn't feel like she had much in common with their strict rules and hierarchy.

But now, as they stepped off the boat, Sella felt that nothing could have adequately prepared her for the difference between this place and her home.

She spent a decade traveling around her island, learning and exploring, helping people where she could, before she returned home to Marra. But no matter where she went in Orakan, it was lush with muted greens, tall trees that reached for the low gray clouds. It was rainy and cold. And when it wasn't cold it was still crisp. The air always felt fresh and clear.

Here, she was met with a brilliantly colored sky, and a strange heat on her skin as the sun set behind them. The sky was expansive, greater than she had ever seen it before. She felt small under it here, as though she was just a little bug among other little bugs, lost under the greatness of it all.

The long dock was crowded with people rushing about them. A few other boats landed, or were about to set out along the shore, their sails set high in bright colors contrasting the sky.

Cali led the way off the dock and to the bustling street ahead, more confident than Sella had seen her in a long time. She hurried to keep the pace with her until they stopped at the edge of the road where tall tan buildings lined the way. Cali turned to her with a bright smile as Lohrna and Beejee caught up and looked out at the crowd with them.

Beside her, Lohrna stood with her mouth hanging open and a few humans passing by stared back at her with equal fascination. Their eyes moved over Sella, to her small horns just above her pointed ears, then found their way to Lohrna, lingering on her antlers that reached up to the sky, tangling her black curly hair. She didn't seem to notice, or at least, didn't seem to mind the attention. She was busy gawking at everything she laid eyes on.

Cali's hand, faint and cold, slipped into Sella's. She squeezed, but her hand pressed through and she reached again, this time, holding Sella delicately. "Welcome to Tollintal," she said as her smile widened.

A rush of warmth started at Sella's fingertips and raced up her arms and to her chest. She smiled back. "Feel good to be home?" Sella asked quietly.

Cali moved closer. "Home is where you are."

"Home is where food is," Beejee said. He pressed his head against Sella's leg, both a kind gesture, and a nudge to get her moving, she was sure.

Cali let Sella go. She clapped her hands once as she raised a single brow. "Oh! You have to try a crushed ice here. It's delicious! Come on, let's find a vendor!"

Sella translated for Lohrna quickly.

"Crushed ice?" her friend repeated. "How do they get ice here? It's sweltering!" She fanned herself with her hand dramatically for greater effect. "I don't know how you lived like this for so long, Cal. I think I'm going to dry out…"

Cali laughed. "It's a spell. Witches are more common here. Many of them perform simple magic, or at least, they have made it their speciality. It's great! They crush up the ice and pour fruit mixes on top. There's so many flavors!"

Sella explained, making a mental note to try to find that spell. She wasn't exactly sure there would be a market for crushed ice in Marra, but on days when sun was out, she thought it might be a nice surprise to make for Cali, even if she couldn't eat it.

Lohrna nodded. "Count me in! I need something to cool me down and settle this stomach." She looked around them quickly, darting her head like a flag in the wind. Her curls got even more caught up in her antlers as she did, making her look wild and catching even more curiosity of the travelers around them. "How far is it to the shops?" she asked.

"Just down the road," Cali said with a wave that Lohnra could not see. She moved between two close buildings, and Sella gestured for Lohrna to follow.

As the group exited the little alleyway, they came

upon a bustling open market, nestled comfortably among the taller clay buildings. Vendors in wooden booths called out to customers, who mingled about, buying treats and trinkets before their long journeys. It reminded Sella of their own square in Marra, except that their port town was usually only a single person or two getting off the ship, staying in the strange hotel for a night, then moving on. Here, it was busy and bright and so very much… alive.

A pain struck Sella but she did her best to mask it with a kind smile. "Come here, Beejee," she said as she leaned down to scoop the tabby cat up into her arms.

He pressed his two front paws against her chest in fake protest, but as he settled down into her collarbone, she knew her instincts had been correct. Someone bumped into Lohrna's shoulder, and she nudged up to Sella in reaction. It was crowded and loud and just a little hazardous to a small familiar.

Lohrna laughed and rubbed her shoulder. "Not even an apology, huh?" she said, though humor prevailed in her tone.

Cali leaned in a little. "Sorry," she said for the other human. She looked up at Sella. "I should have warned you," she said. "Humans are… in a hurry. Perhaps because we don't live as long."

Sella pulled Beejee in closer. It was true that humans had short lives compared to Wyldes, but… somehow that made the tragedy of Cali's death all the more heartbreaking. Such a short time here, and what she had was taken. She did her best to not let it show. She squared her shoulders and stood on her toes to see over the heads of the quickly moving people.

"This way!" Cali called as she moved like water within the crowd. "We'll get a crushed ice, then make our way to the cart station."

As if she heard the ghost, Lohrna pulled out a folded paper from her pocket. "Well, Sediri's instructions say that the town is close to here at least. I'm done with travel, to be honest. Do you think the carts are going to be bumpy?"

"Can we skip the ice?" Beejee grumbled into Sella's neck, ignoring Lohrna entirely. "I just want to get out of this crowd and grab some chicken."

"We'll find something for you to eat," Sella said. Her gaze followed the row of vendors until she found a woman in a broad hat handing out what looked like a mountain of snow in a bowl, topped with glistening pink and purple fruits. Beside her, another woman was preparing meat over an open fire.

They ordered, with Lohrna fumbling her way through the interaction. First, she held out her hand as a greeting but the human kitchen witch declined, citing cleanliness. Then, she sampled every fruit, going back to the first one twice and still waited until Beejee scolded her before she made a decision.

With Lohrna's ice in hand, and Sella feeding Beejee bits of unseasoned meat, they journeyed away from the square and out of the crowds just as the sun began to set.

With her fruit and ice in one hand, and the notes from Sediri in the other, Lohrna led the way to the edge of town, to a set of stables where a human waited at the gate.

He was leaning on the fencing with his arms crossed and a bored expression on his face.

Still, Lohrna bounded up to him, stuffing the paper back into her pocket and her mouth full of ice. "Hi," she said loudly from the side of her mouth.

"You're here for a ride to Sunfall?" he asked, skipping pleasantries.

Cali leaned in and whispered, "Alright, this is abnormally rude. Not at all the way we typically are."

"Yep!" Lohrna said, unfazed by his attitude. "Sediri sent us. We have a cart here, right?"

The man nodded behind him toward the stables where a simple cart with two horses were already fastened with leather leads.

Sella had heard of horses before, but had never actually seen one. She let Beejee down and looked them over with wide eyes. "How long is the journey?" she asked, her eyes still fixed on the spotted horses.

"We'll be there by morning," he said. "But only barely. You *were* late. Come on. We have to get going."

Sella sighed.

THE NIGHT AIR was much cooler now that the sun had disappeared long ago. The back of the cart was hard and the group jostled every now and then when there was a crack or bump on the path. Still, Sella smiled.

Cali's head rested on her shoulder, Beejee curled up

on her lap. Lohrna lay on the floor of the cart, she used her arms as a pillow and stared up at the starfilled sky.

Sella followed her gaze to the sky. It was full of more stars than she had ever seen. Each shining dot illuminated brightly all across the black sky.

"Have you ever seen anything like this on your travels?" Lohrna asked in a small whisper.

"Nothing so… immense," she said quietly. "I feel…"

"Small?" Lohrna finished for her.

Sella nodded gently. She looked to Cali, then Beejee. And yet, she felt infinite.

THREE

The Recipe Book is Wrong

Sediri had described Sunfall as a lively town full of potential clients. But what Sella saw upon their early morning arrival had been a tiny town with mostly empty streets and small buildings in neat little rows. They met no one but Sediri so far, and she had ushered them inside the little shop before anything else had opened. It felt almost desolate and empty, or at least, so much smaller and quieter than any town she had been to.

Still, the outside of the building was strangely reminiscent of the storefront in Marra. A two story building, with a living space above the little shop. Two large windows facing out at the ground level with a sign posted reading 'Certified Kitchen Witch, Credentials Available Upon Request, Inquire Within for Daily Offerings' hung. In big golden lettering between the first floor and the second, the shop's name 'Black Feather Potions & Pastries' glimmered in the early morning light.

Inside the shop, still mostly unpacked, Sella furrowed

her brow at the old book in front of her for a moment before her eyes shifted, slightly, to Sediri. "This recipe book is…" she began.

"Garbage," Beejee finished for her.

Sella cast him a quick narrowed eye. "Not exactly," she said, trying to dispel the obvious tension between them. "But…"

Sediri put a hand on her hip. She waited.

Sediri, the other kitchen witch from Marra, had hired her to come and help her open her shop amongst the humans months ago. It had taken them longer to arrive than Sediri thought it would, and Sella had also hoped that Sediri would have done more around the new shop by now. Sediri hired her to help set up, certainly, but she had emphasized the need for help with her signature recipe especially. And Sella was hopeful that was going to be the bulk of her labor. But to no avail. Sediri had hired them and seemed to be determined to use them for everything they had stipulated prior to their arrival.

Lohrna would, in fact, be setting up and decorating most of the shop, and Sella needed to create a luck spell.

No one in Tollintal had anything like it, Sediri had explained. Though no one in Orakan did either, Sella wanted to counter. And while the tome Sediri had from her family did have a recipe… It was complicated. Far more complicated than she had led on.

Sella couldn't help but feel a little tricked, though she knew in her heart she was just wishing she'd have more free time to find Cali a spell for speaking. It seemed that her luck had run out long ago and she'd need to work especially hard for this as well.

Meanwhile, Beejee didn't think Sediri, or her grackle familiar, deserved their help. He made it clear by sitting on the counter with his tail thumping loudly on the wood and his ears pulled back, clearly annoyed.

Sella wanted to shoo him away. He had been happy enough with the up front payment, after his negotiations, of course. And the stake in the shop didn't hurt either. Passive income was always nice, he has told Sella. So, in her opinion, both of them ought to be feeling a little more grateful and a little less frustrated that work did, in fact, require work.

Still, as Sella examined the spell before her, she couldn't help but think it wouldn't work. The ingredients didn't seem quite right. For a luck spell, something was definitely off about it.

"I'm leaving tomorrow, Sella," Sediri reminded her with a flick of her wrist. The black bird on her shoulder flapped his wings as if punctuating her statement.

Beejee hissed at the grackle. "You're lucky you're traveling at all and not locked up in a jail cell."

"That's true," Cali said as she materialized between the two witches.

Both jumped at her sudden arrival. Sella, however, was used to Cali's sudden appearances and recovered quickly, while Sediri kept her hand over her heart, her eyes wide.

She finally straightened her dress and lifted her chin

up as though nothing had happened. "You are being paid," Sediri said, her composure back.

Cali rolled her eyes, crossing her arms over her chest dramatically. She looked at Sediri with a cocked head. "You want a luck spell? You'll get it before you get back. Sella can make it," she said, as if it was a challenge. Around her, her auburn hair moved slightly as if a breeze had blown into the room, a sure sign that Cali was about to get angry.

Sella wanted to sink into the floor. Cali always seemed to think that Sella could do anything. And while she was a gifted witch, she wasn't *that* good. After all, there was, of course, *The Incident* no one in her hometown would be quiet about. And that was decades ago. But, instead of fighting it, Sella pushed her shoulders back and nodded. "I'll do my best," she said.

Sediri glared at Beejee, then her eyes flicked to Sella. "I would like the shop operational by the time I get back," she said.

"It will be," Sella said. "But I can't promise a spell to give the drinker good luck will be perfected by then. Sediri, this recipe book is old and out of date. If I use some of these ingredients, you'll end up in the same position you were in before."

It wasn't long ago that Sediri, while working for a company that specialized in kitchen witchery, opened her own shop in Sella's town and tried to run her out of business. Of course, talk of the town was quick to notice that the company's recipes weren't very potent, and there were occasional bad side effects. Most notably, confusion, disorientation, fever, and a nasty rash. Which… *may have* partly contributed to the death of a prominent local official.

Sella couldn't take the risk of something like that happening to someone here, or anyone who took one of her blends.

Beejee still didn't feel that Sediri truly got her dues, and Sella found herself agreeing with him from time to time. Justice wasn't easy or even, it seemed, fair sometimes.

Sediri tossed a lock of red hair over her shoulder. Her familiar squawked at her, dodging the hair as best he could. She shook her head, dismissing him. "I have faith in you, Sella. Don't make me say it again," she grumbled at last.

Sella sighed. She glanced at Cali who was smiling brightly back at her as if they had won a fight. "I'll see what I can do," Sella said at last.

Sediri's eyes softened, just a little. "Thank you."

THE NEXT MORNING, Lohrna was busy bouncing around the store, unpacking crate after crate. She examined each book, each little statue, every single mug and jar as she set them down gently in little categories along the dark wood floor. Occasionally, she would show off a trinket to Sella, or Beejee.

Beejee would pretend not to care, but wander over to her as though he just happened to be going that direction anyway and then they would talk about what the value of the item might be or if it was purely sentimental and where it would look best, behind the bar, or on a shelf?

Sella watched from the corner of her eye as Lohrna would point to one direction, only for her familiar to shake his little head slowly and raise a paw to the opposite direction.

Little fires overhead drifted along the ceiling, careful to not get too close to the wood above. Still, they provided some much needed extra light. Though the front windows let in an abundance of sunlight, it was still shadowy at the back of the shop, especially, below the counter where Sella mostly spent the day organizing rows of potions and powders and pre-made remedies.

Cali sat on the counter, her legs swinging back and forth as she recounted to Sella the descriptions of every human who walked by. And even some who cupped their hands and looked within the windows. "A short man… bald," she said. "A woman next to him with long braids… Oh! She's hitting him in the arm to keep moving. I wonder if he usually is the curious one or if she's just more subtle."

Sella peeked up from behind the counter. They were leaving now, nothing but shadows in the window until they were gone from sight. She wondered if the town was awake now, and if the talk about them moving in was positive or full of distrust. It really could go either way, she figured. And she wasn't exactly in a hurry to figure it out.

FOUR

The Shadow

"Let's get a move on it," Beejee ordered.

They were all above the shop, sitting around the rectangular table with cold teas in front of them. Sella was glaring into her cup. She had stayed up all night working on the luck recipe, but she didn't feel any luckier than she had the night before. All she felt was tired.

She had traded ingredients out, played with proportions, but nothing worked. The spell was bordering on impossible.

The early morning light filtered through the three small windows that overlooked the quiet travertine paved street. It cast light shadows along the dark wood floor and illuminated the cool tan clay of the walls with a slight glow. As Sella squinted at the wall closest to her, she noticed that within the clay were flecks of minerals of some kind. They sparkled when they caught the light, illuminating the space with what looked like a touch of magic.

A crumble of thick, heavy blankets were piled at the foot of the bed. They were a lovely pattern, a zig zag of yellows and reds that matched the sunrise outside. But they were too warm for Sella and when she finally tried settling into bed, she was surprised that they were so heavy despite the warm night.

Still, it had provided a space for Lohrna to curl up, as she preferred sleeping in the smallest possible position while Sella sprawled out. It had been that way since they were children, when Lohrna would practically drag Sella from her own home, calling back to the witch's mother that if it was alright with her, she'd drop her off in the morning.

Sella had always been hesitant to leave, afraid, though she was never sure of what. But it was never a wasted evening and she was happy her friend pushed her to do things she wouldn't usually. Even now, Sella was glad that Lohrna was there with her, sleeping in like they had done when they were children.

They only had the one bed, but it was large enough for all of them, though Sella hoped they wouldn't be here long. She wanted to do her duty to Sediri and then move on.

Finding a spell to help Cali speak with top priority, and everything she did here was hinging on that making it all worth it.

"What's the rush?" Lohrna leaned back in her chair, letting her head fall over the pale wooden backing.

The familiar huffed, a hissing sound. "I'd like to get going before it gets too hot," he said.

Lohrna lifted her head. "I thought cats liked warmth," she teased.

Beejee's eyes narrowed. "We traded one small town for another," he said bluntly. "We won't find what we need here."

Sella's gaze shifted to him. He was right. She had come to this town for a range of reasons. To help Sediri, yes. To get paid more than she could dream didn't hurt either. To grant Beejee his wish to travel. To get to know Cali's home. But, if she was honest with herself, it was mostly to gather more knowledge. There was a spell out there to make it so Cali could communicate with people other than witches. She knew it. She just had to find it.

And Beejee was right again. It wasn't going to be in another small town.

Their ticket back home was one they couldn't postpone and they couldn't afford to buy another. Their time was finite.

She sighed as a heavy feeling settled into her bones.

At the same time, just traveling about the new land without knowing where they were going didn't seem like it would be all too productive either. She was tired of feeling like she was running in circles. Going fast and going nowhere.

Cali leaned in. "Well, we only have a few days off during our time here. Sediri is certainly making us work for it."

Beejee stomped his foot, his claws made a hollow little sound on the table. "All the more reason to get going," he said.

"Alright, alright," Lohrna groaned, sitting up straighter. She hadn't heard what Cali said, but Beejee's unrelenting instance seemed enough to convince her at last. "Let me finish my tea and then we'll ask around and see where we can go for some good old fashioned exploration."

Beejee's ear twitched. His gold eyes fixed on the three little windows on the wall just as they started the rattle, a low urgent sound like fingers tapping to get their attention.

The group turned to the windows as Sella rose. She moved closer to inspect the sound and their vibrations grew more insistent. "High winds," she said quietly as she squinted out into the sunlight. It was too bright to see, then, suddenly, they were drenched in shadow.

"What—" Sella began.

"Wyverns," Cali whispered.

FIVE

The Wyvern Riders

"Wyverns!" Lohrna stood so quickly that her chair knocked back with a loud crack on the floor. She rushed to the window with a smile so wide, it took up her whole face. She turned back to Sella, already pulling on her long sleeves like a child trying to get her to follow her. "Sella! Wyverns! Let's go see!"

Sella turned to Cali.

The ghost's eyes were wide, and her shoulders slumped inward. "This isn't a good thing, Sella," Cali said quietly, as if she was afraid of smashing Lohrna's excitement. "There's no good reason for the military to be here."

Sella's brow furrowed. Her stomach sank slowly as a feeling of cold dread washed over her. She was unaccustomed to human culture, human customs. A misstep here and there with a human in the shop would be embarrassing. A misstep with a giant beast involved… that felt much more high stakes.

Lohrna, however, seemed too excited to notice Sella's sudden shift. She was already at the door, hand on the brass handle. "Let's go see them!" she called, throwing the door open and bounding down the narrow stairs as quickly as she safely could.

Beejee's back bristled, his gray striped fur rising slightly. He looked up at Sella. "Come on, we better make sure she doesn't get lit on fire."

Sella felt a shiver run down her arms.

"Don't worry," Cali said as she followed Sella and Beejee down the stairs. "Most wyvern don't breathe fire."

Sella shook her head. "Well, that's something," she mumbled back.

Cali pushed her shoulder into Sella's on their way down. It was a playful gesture, and Sella felt a rush of warmth in her cheeks.

Cali's shoulder was somewhat solid. It wasn't always.

Lohrna waited by the front door of the shop. She looked back at Sella, then to Beejee. "Ready?"

Cali's hand slipped into Sella's. She squeezed it gently, then shimmered out of view. "I'll be right here," her voice whispered from all around.

Beejee let out a huff, then stood by Lohrna's feet. "Let's meet these beasts," he said.

Lohrna nodded, then opened the door, letting a cascade of bright sunlight spill into the room.

Sella blinked furiously as her eyes adjusted to the sudden light.

The wind had calmed. The air was still and already growing warm despite the early morning. A few owners of the stores along the street had come out of their businesses, filling the street with chatter. Wyverns, it seemed, though native to Tollintal, were uncommon enough, at least in a small town like this, that everyone journeyed out and set aside their morning tasks to see them.

Sella followed Lohrna and Beejee down the road, moving together with the few other store owners as they all made their way to the end of the street and into the large open air market.

The paved square was empty of the usual night market booths that Sediri had told them about. The bright color textiles, beads hanging from canopies, all the hustle, was put away. In their place, three huge mythical looking animals stretched toward the sky on their legs. The riders on their backs held their hands over their faces to block out the sun as they looked out into the streets, surveying the crowd as if looking for someone in particular.

Sella has seen wyverns in books before. She'd seen them on Cali's embroidered tea towel. She'd heard stories. But just like everything here, none of that was adequate preparation for what stood before her.

The three wyverns were massive.

As they stood on two powerful, scaled legs, their heads nearly reached the top of the low buildings. Scaled, armor-like skin sparkled in the sunlight, shimmering with every quiver and flex of their strong muscles beneath. Bat-like wings, dark brown leather with sharp hooked claws at the ends like broken hands, beat slowly as if they were stretching after their flight.

The largest, the one in the middle, bowed its head low to look closer at the people gathering around them. Horns over its brows cast dark shadows over large reptile eyes. It grimaced, or perhaps smiled, showing off a row of dagger sharp teeth. Its tail whipped around its legs quickly, revealing black spikes that ran along its back and down to the tip of its tail.

Sella's eyes moved up its snout and down the long neck to a man who sat upright on its back. He was holding a set of leather reins with a loose grip, dressed in tight-fitting clothes, the same brown as his wyvern's wings, with a few shining patches of metal attached to the front over his heart.

She squinted, trying to see more clearly from her safe distance. It didn't look like armor. More like decorations.

She was unfamiliar with the king's guard in her own island, luckily having never any kind of run in with them. She had no concept of what was normal or not in the military, but judging by the blank uniforms of the other two, this one in the middle must be the one in charge.

She looked around for Cali, but she was nowhere to be found. Perhaps the scene before them was just too much for her. Or she was doing reconnaissance elsewhere.

Sella's fingers twitched. They warmed slightly, ready to ignite in flames.

Beside her, Lohrna nearly jumped as she suddenly grabbed Sella's arm. "Are you seeing this?" she gasped.

Around them, people clustered together. Some hung on one another the way Lohrna held Sella now. While others pointed boldly at the beasts with anger in their expressions. Still, no one went close to them. Everyone kept a wide radius around them and Sella realized that without meaning to, she and Beejee had both taken a few steps back into the crowd, pulling Lohrna along with them.

But Lohrna's eyes were fixed in fascination at the scene before them. She was wide eyed, almost joyous, as her eyes ran up and down the wyvern in the middle, a blue-tinted one who looked around with a low growl, loud enough to break the din of the crowds, but still just below a level Sella was comfortable with.

She grabbed Lohrna's hand and brought her closer to her. Something about these creatures, besides their massive stature and deadly appearance, made Sella uneasy. Perhaps it was the reaction of the town. No one seemed excited they were here, and somehow, Sella thought it might be less unnerving if the wyverns had come in growling and hissing and teeth barred.

Their steady, calculated movements, was like a fire waiting to spread.

A few groups backed away, but two remained. A shorter bald man and a woman with long braids down her back. Sella recognized their description as the ones that Cali must have seen the day before.

The woman crossed her arms and cocked her head casually. She stared directly at the man in the middle. "What an honor to have the high command once again in our humble little town," she said. Her tone was mocking, almost silly. Though from her expression and the scowl on the man's face, she meant it as a challenge. "What brings you to Sunfall?"

The man on the blue wyvern settled in his seat. He let go of the reins and the beast below him shook its head fiercely. "We're here for lodging," he said, his voice bold, as if alerting the entire town and not just answering the woman before him. "Just passing through."

The woman nodded down an alleyway. "Right, then you know where to go," she said. She turned to the crowds of people and waved her hands, ushering everyone to disperse. "Move along," she called to everyone. "Come on now, nothing to see here."

Lohrna's eyes shifted from the woman back to the wyverns. She and Sella were still gripping each other's arms gently.

"Let's go," Sella whispered as the rest of the groups began to filter away. "Lohr, let's go."

Lohrna nodded at last, peeling her gaze from the group and dropping Sella's arm. "Alright," she said quietly. "But they sure are beautiful, aren't they?"

Beautiful, Sella thought, the way a storm was. The way a wildfire was. Beautiful in its possibility of destruction. Beautiful in the way it made her feel incredibly small and unsafe in a world where she had always been the one everyone else feared.

SIX

The Other Witch

"WELL, THERE GOES OUR DAY OFF," Beejee grumbled from his perch on the counter as Sella turned the Black Feather Potions & Pastries shop sign to open.

"Beejee, we just saw giant *wyverns*," Lohrna said, busy opening a crate at the front of the shop. She inspected the contents of the crate with a raised brow, then turned to him. "And all you can think about is your day off?"

Beejee thrust his head to one side. "Yes," he said. "We have too many other things to worry about. Like," he turned his attention to Sella, "are you going to be selling the special blend?"

Sella rolled her neck and prepared the pot of coffee. "It's worth a try," she said. "Who knows, maybe we'll get lucky and it actually works?"

"When are we ever lucky?" Beejee scoffed.

Lohrna shook her head. "Such little faith," she said. "Did you see people's faces when they showed up? Folks will be in need of some calm and cozy blends, anyway. It's our *duty* to open up for them."

Sella looked up from her place behind the counter. She had her hands wrapped around the metal pot, trying to infuse all the good luck she could into the ingredients she had added. It warmed at her touch and a little steam escaped the spout as the room filled with the comforting scent of cinnamon and clove. She released her hands and ducked behind the counter.

Better add something extra, she thought. Just in case the luck was nothing more than a spicy addition. She grabbed a jar filled with orange liquid and added a few drops of joy to the pot.

An aroma of bright citrus mixed with the spices and Lohrna and Cali both sighed, the sound of relief.

Still, Cali sat on a barstool with her head in her hand. "I don't like the wyverns here," she said solemnly. "Nothing good can come of this."

"Speaking of little faith," Beejee said as his tail flicked.

"Are you worried?" Sella asked.

Cali sighed out again. "Not worried… just. Mildly concerned?"

Somehow, that felt worse.

The shop door opened and Lohrna hopped aside as two soldiers walked in. She smiled at them, but they paid her little mind, though the shorter one gave her a simple nod on his way past.

Sella recognized them as the two lower ranking men.

She exchanged a glance with Cali who disappeared from view as her voice whispered, "Remember, shake hands twice and then get to business. Soldiers don't do small talk."

Sella nodded once and then put on her best customer service grin. She hoped it looked natural, though anxiety crept into her brows. "Good morning," she said brightly, extending her hand.

Each soldier took it, gave exactly two quick shakes, and then looked around them.

"Is there a menu?" the shorter one asked.

Sella shook her head. "We're still in the soft launch phase. We are opening this shop to help out a fellow kitchen witch."

His eyes moved over her horns, but he didn't ask any follow up questions.

Just passing through, Sella thought. *No small talk.*

"Do you have travel ceramic?" the taller one asked. His stare was hard and cold.

Sella shivered, but hid it with a tuck of her hair behind her pointed ear. "Not yet," she said. She poured two cups of steaming coffee anyway. "On us this time. It's the daily special."

Neither asked what that meant, instead, they took their mugs and breathed in deeply. At least neither seemed to question her intentions or that a cat was perched on the counter, eyeing them suspiciously.

"Long flight?" Lohrna called from the front of the shop. "I've never seen anything like that before. In

Orakan, we don't have any wyverns. Or military… not really."

They both turned to her, the taller soldier sipped from his mug while the shorter soldier smiled at her, creases forming along his cheeks as he did. "We try not to ride them too hard," he said kindly.

Lohrna smiled back but took her cue that the conversation was over before it began. She went back to work unpacking her crate, organizing the trinkets within on the little table.

The men finished their drinks quickly, and, to Sella's satisfaction, looked as though they desperately needed it. It may not have been a long journey, but Sella felt that it was a difficult one nonetheless.

As their postures lightened and a hint of a smile fell upon the taller man's face, Sella felt pride swell up into her chest. Lohrna was right. It was their job to bring this kind of warmth and comfort to where they could.

A FEW OTHER villagers stopped in throughout the day, though after the soldiers had requested, and to Beejee's great pleasure, paid for their second round of drinks, she improvised by selling 'Don't Strangle People', a popular blend of calm, focus, and a hefty dose of patience.

She listened for any gossip about the wyverns but most people instead, asked her questions about the shop, where she was from, who was running it, and if there would be any pastries as the sign advertised.

"Orakan, across the sea."

"Sediri, a kitchen witch you may have met previously." The town was small enough, certainly.

And, "Yes, I just didn't expect to be open today. Scones and biscuits will be available soon."

Meanwhile, Lohrna moved and removed items from the long shelves, tilting her head this way and that to try to get the perfect placement of the various little decorations that Sediri had brought with her.

She spent most of the day also asking questions, though it was more her speculating aloud about how long the wyverns would be in town, who that woman was who took charge in the square, and when they'd close so she could decompress in the tavern after the long day of decorating.

Sella pinched her brow as the sun began to set.

Cali sparkled into view beside her. "Long day?" she asked.

Sella lowered her hand and smiled at her. "Every day is a good day that ends with you," she whispered. "What did you get up to today?"

"Snooping on the military," she said. "I'd make an excellent spy. They should recruit me."

"Learn anything interesting?"

"Just that their squad commander is kind of a prickly one," she said. "He was barking orders at the others and the wyverns all day."

Sella hummed. That sounded about right.

"Alright," Lohrna called as she stretched her arms up

over head. "Let's close up. I'm ready to get out of here and never look at this shelf again."

"Where to?" Cali asked.

"To the tavern?" Sella asked Lohrna and Cali.

Cali shook her head. "The owner is a witch," she said. "I learned that from overhearing the soldiers talk. Their leader *does not* like her."

Sella's brows rose. "Anything I should know?"

"Nothing I could figure out," she said. "I think he's just a prejudiced old fool."

A small chuckle escaped Sella's throat. She turned to Lohrna. "The tavern owner is a witch," she said. "Apparently, she doesn't get along with the other soldier."

Lohrna rubbed her hands together. "Small town drama!" she hissed wickedly. "Come on, let's go."

"See you upstairs," Sella said to Cali.

"I'll stay too," Beejee said as he jumped from his little bed on the counter.

The ghost stood on her toes, her feet an inch off the floor, and placed a gentle kiss on Sella's brow. "Be careful, have fun."

Sella's cheeks flushed.

Lohrna waved her hand. "Plenty of time for that later," she said with a grin as she noticed the redness in Sella's face.

Sella laughed and with a flick of her wrist, the fires in the shop extinguished and the sign flipped to 'Closed'.

THE TAVERN WAS CROWDED.

Sella wasn't sure if it was always like this or if the wyvern's arrival had sparked everyone's need to flock together. Sella resolved to not linger. One drink, say hello to the barkeep, and she was going to be out of there.

Lohrna, on the other hand, looked elated with the noise and the people, most of whom gave them both a wide berth, side eyeing their antlers and horns but saying nothing. She led the way through the crowd with confidence Sella could not muster, and squeezed her way to the end of the bar, practically pulling Sella by her elbow to fit.

The barkeep smiled at them and motioned that she'd be a moment.

Sella's shoulders slumped.

"Reminds me of Hazen's," Lohrna said through the din around them.

Sella's eyes moved over the tavern.

It was smaller and almost completely different decor, tables, and candles. She had been to taverns all around their home island and this one was just the same and just as different as the rest of them. Still, she smiled at her friend and said, "Sure does."

Lohrna had never left their small town until now and the last thing Sella wanted to do was make her feel self-conscious about it. Especially since Sella was the one who had left so long ago and Lohrna still seemed occasionally bitter about it.

Rightfully so, Sella thought as the other witch finally made it to their end of the bar.

"You're the new kitchen witch Sediri was telling me about," she said warmly to Lohrna.

Her friend shook her head. "I'm just the decorator," she said with a smile. "I'm Lohrna, this is Sella, the kitchen witch."

Sella held out her hand and the woman took it firmly.

"Call me Verol," she said. "That's my short name. I'm the owner here and also a witch. It's good to have another in town. Can't have too many."

"A kitchen witch?" Sella asked.

Verol smiled and shook her head. "No, I specialize in growing plants and herbs. It doesn't help with business here much, but it is a helpful skill in the desert."

"Verolanishi!" a man called loudly at the other end of the bar.

Verol rolled her eyes dramatically, making sure he saw. "One moment!" she called back. She turned back to Lohrna with a little tilt of her head. "What can I get you?"

"Red wine?" Lohrna asked.

Verol nodded. "Of course," she said. "Vintage, too. Folks here tend to prefer the stronger stuff. Here's a friendly tip," she turned to Sella, "make your coffees extra bitter. We like those flavors here."

"Will do," Sella said with a smile.

"A bottle of our finest red wine," Verol said a bit louder with a gesture at her forehead that Sella didn't quite understand the meaning of. "On the house as a welcome, but don't expect it every time." Her laughter followed her down the bar as she grabbed two mugs and an ancient looking bottle from below the counter.

She seemed kind and warm, friendly. Sella wondered for a moment if maybe Cali had misheard before. She couldn't imagine someone not getting along with her.

"Strange place," she said under her breath and she and Lohrna sipped their drinks, alone in a sea of people.

SEVEN

Fire in the Forge

"SELLA!" Beejee yowled loudly. His two front paws pressed painfully into Sella's chest.

She opened her eyes to see her familiar's face pushed up against hers. His whiskers tickled her cheeks and she shoved him back gently, blinking and coughing a little as awareness crept into her body and mind. "What?" she grumbled, sitting up slowly and rubbing her eye with the back of one hand. "What happened now?"

Beejee paced along the side of the bed. He looked from the window, to the still sleeping Lohrna at the foot of the bed, then back to Sella. "Something terrible happened."

Sella yawned. Something terrible woke her up again too soon. This was becoming a pattern. "What happened?" she repeated as the fog of sleep finally began to dissipate from the forefront of her mind.

"I heard something," Beejee said. His pacing suddenly

stilled and he nearly bounded back to her, his feet once again resting on her collarbone. "I heard a fire blast."

Sella pushed him off again. "A fire blast?"

An indent in the pillow beside her deepened before Cali shimmered into view. "A fire blast?" she echoed.

Beejee hissed. He raced to one of the small windows, pressing his nose to the glass so it left a wet imprint. "A fire blast," he said. "I think something is happening. It can't be good."

Cali was gone in a blink before popping back up at the window as well. She looked out with Beejee. "I don't see anything…" she whispered, as if afraid of waking the still snoring Lohrna. She glanced back at Sella, then squared her shoulders. "Stay here, you two. I'll go check it out."

"Wait—" Sella reached for her but she was gone in a flicker.

Beejee hurried back to Sella's side. The two waited in silence for a long while as Sella struggled to stretch out her shoulders.

This bed wasn't home. She was sleeping poorly and no matter how much she tried, she was tired.

They waited for a few moments, listening to Lohrna's heavy breathing. Sella rolled her neck and Beejee paced at the door, though both knew that wasn't how Cali would come back in.

And just as she had that thought, Cali appeared in the middle of the room, her hair and skirt blowing around her as if she had plunged herself in water. "It's not good…" she said quickly. Her hair whipped around her face. "Wake Lohrna up."

SELLA'S HEART was beating hard against her ribs as she prepared the group a pot of warm coffee in the kitchen. Lohrna and Beejee and Cali sat at the table, each eagerly awaiting either the caffeine or the smell of spells. Sella had managed to put a spare sheet over Cali's head, but there were no glasses to be found in the small room above the shop. She was angry at herself for not thinking of packing a pair for her.

But her form beneath the sheet was still visible, giving Lohrna something to look at, at least.

Sella couldn't be worried about her forgetfulness now. She wrapped her hands around the pot and breathed in as slowly as she could. *Calm. Love. Family…* she poured her intentions into the brew, though she knew some of her anxiety would inevitably make it in no matter how she tried to keep it together for them.

Someone was dead, and it was only a matter of time until the little town woke up and discovered him. As far as Sella could tell, a prominent member of the military had just died the very night they arrived in a town that they weren't particularly welcome. He had been burned, so swiftly and so quickly that he probably hadn't even seen it coming.

And Sella, new in town with no connections or affections, had a powerful affinity for fire. It was a terrible position to be and she had to fight every urge to simply pack a bag and flee with her friends back home.

She sighed and shook her head at the pot of coffee. It'd have to do.

Sella brought the pot to the table and poured three mugs, nearly overflowing the last one as her mind slipped away from the task at hand. She steadied her arm and set the pot aside.

From under the sheet, Cali shifted a bit to smell the steam. "Hmmm." It was an ambivalent sound, like she wasn't quite sure if the coffee would help or hurt.

Sella's expression soured, but just for a moment. She sat down and pulled her own mug closer to her, careful to keep her face stoic. She didn't want to upset Cali anymore than she already was.

"Sooooo," Lohrna finally broke the tension in the room with a sing-song tone. "We're awfully unlucky."

Cali laughed, the sheet rippled a little as she did and Lohrna smiled back.

"Right?" Lohrna held her mug aloft, a motion of comradery with the ghost. "Any chance it was an accident?'

Cali shook her head.

Lohrna deflated. "Yeah, burnt to a crisp doesn't seem accidental, even if he was in a forge."

"Though being there does help us," Sella said, almost to herself. Only Cali seemed to notice. Her head turned to her slightly beneath the sheet.

"At least it was probably quick," Cali said definitively.

"Beejee heard the fire but no scream… And to be so severely… Well. At least it was quick."

Lohrna went on, unaware of Cali's comment. "What are the odds this little town has a murder the night that a bunch of wyverns come to town. No chance he's coming back as a ghost, huh?"

Cali shrugged. She leaned down, back into the warmth of the silver steam.

Sella sighed until her lungs went empty. She took a long sip, then leaned back in her chair. "Well, the death of a prominent member of the military probably means we're not on consulting duty. They'll probably bring in a detective, right?"

Cali nodded. "A military authorized one, I'm sure. They have their own rules and trials and things."

"Not that our Orakan papers would mean anything here," Sella grumbled.

Beejee pressed a paw to her arm. "You need to watch your fire."

Sella closed her eyes slowly as the slow, drowning feeling took hold of her heart, encasing it in cold and crushing weight. He was right, and it was already something she had begun to worry about. She had no motive, but she was new in town, transient, and a witch. The amount of trouble this would give her probably heavily depended on how open to foreigners the detective and the town were.

Bitterly, her thoughts began to swirl around her, clouding her mind like a heavy fog until she was lost in it. She wasn't sure which way was out.

Lohrna smiled, though her brows were furrowed still. "Hey, I'm sure it'll be fine," she said. "Besides, once they see how helpful we are, we can lead up another investigation. We'll be heroes!"

"I say we skip town before anyone wakes up," Beejee countered, vocalizing the darkest part of Sella's thoughts. "This doesn't end well for us."

Lohrna rolled her eyes, though her expression turned playful. "Beejee, what about helping out? We're capable. We can bring justice to this town."

"Our ticket back home isn't for a while," Sella thought aloud. "It's not as if we could get far on foot. And we don't exactly blend in."

Beejee barred his teeth. "We're getting dragged into another mystery, aren't we?"

EIGHT

Once for 'Yes', Two for 'No'

THE SUN finally rose above the rooftops, coloring the streets in a warm golden glow. Sella had already opened the shop and brewed a large batch of calming blend. It would seem a bit suspicious, perhaps, that they were open early and only on the second day of a relatively soft launch, but Cali and Lohrna had assured her it was the right thing to do.

Much to Beejee's distress.

He paced along the counter, mumbling occasionally about fleeing or scheming ways to make Sella appear to have an affinity for water instead of fire. "We could spill some water, Lohrna could shout, 'ah, there you go again with that darn water!'" He cast her a quick look, though she was not listening at all. He huffed.

Cali sat at a table across from Lohrna listening to her theories patiently with a gentle smile. Every so often, she would reach out and tap Lohrna's arm.

"Hey, I felt that one!" Lohrna said as she shot up taller in her seat. "One for 'yes', two for 'no', alright?"

Sella busied herself with a potion in front of her. She added a small spoonful of yellow powder and the concoction bubbled over, hissing as it spilled onto the wood countertop. "Tides!" Sella swore just as the door to the shop blew open.

"Please tell me you have something to calm my nerves!" the barkeep said as the door hit the wall with a loud *bang*. "Did you hear the news?"

At her feet, the little white cat meowed gently.

Beejee's tail flicked. He hopped off the counter and approached the other familiar with quick feet. "You heard it too?"

The white cat chirped in what seemed like an enthusiastic agreement.

Sella poured a large mug of coffee for Verol. "Calming blend," she said quietly, hoping her demeanor seemed easy, or at least, not guilty. She hoped a fellow witch would understand her trepidation but it was all still new and she wasn't sure how much, if anything to reveal.

Verol grabbed the mug and downed it in several rapid gulps. "Thank goodness we have a kitchen witch here finally," she said at last. Her posture relaxed and she sank into a stool at the bar. She lowered her forearms onto the counter, then turned to the two familiars with a smile. Her eyes shifted over to Cali and Lohrna. "I've never seen a ghost, until you came here," she said, though not unkindly.

Cali sat up straighter. She smiled, wrinkles forming at the corners of her green eyes. "I hope I'm making a good name for us," she said. "I'm sorry this is all happening in your little town."

"I'm not terribly sorry," Verol said at last. "I mean," she turned back to Sella with wide eyes, "that sounded terrible. What I mean is that Baz was always being a bully around here. Coming in and throwing his weight around."

"So someone would have a reason to hurt him?" Lohrna asked.

Verol nodded. "Many would. Though not someone very smart. With Baz gone, it'll bring even more military to town." She looked up at the ceiling. "I don't know how we'll feed any more wyverns… Do you have a spell to make more food?"

Sella shook her head. "That would be useful, though."

"Too bad," Verol said. She slid her mug back across the counter. "More, please."

Lohrna rose, her mug held firmly in her hand. "I'm going to look for clues!"

Sella's eyes widened. "Lohr!" She looked down at the pot of coffee. This was supposed to be a calming blend. What had she done wrong?

"Are you *trying* to make us look guilty?" Beejee said. He moved quickly to block the door, though, given his size, it looked much more like a mild inconvenience than an actual obstacle.

Cali shimmered to Lohrna's side. "I'll go with her,"

she said. "I know this land, the customs here. Besides," she cast a glance at the unaware woman, "Lohrna is charming and fun. People will love her and we could afford to be endeared around here, don't you think?"

Beejee bristled. His eyes shifted to Sella, waiting.

"Cali wants to go with you," she told Lohrna.

"Yes!" Lohrna nearly jumped. "The investigation begins!"

Sella and Verol both cast each other a sideways look. This could end up being her worst decision. Or the one that saved them. She felt like she was standing at the edge of a hull on a dark and starless night. Directionless and alone.

It was true that Lohrna was friendly and never seemed to have any trouble getting along with anyone. On the other hand… "If you go, then bring Beejee," Sella said at last before she could talk herself out of it.

Cali nodded. She beamed at Beejee. "Come on, little buddy!"

"Don't call me little," Beejee said as the three slipped out of the cafe and out into the bright morning light.

Verol shook her head. She leaned over the counter and her familiar joined her, pressing her head against the witch's shoulder. "You have an enthusiastic group here," she said. "Are they always this excited about a muder?"

Sella tucked a lock of choppy hair behind her pointed ear. "Actually, yes, we've had a few mysteries to solve in our hometown and they're always weirdly excited about it."

Verol shuddered. "Well, I guess we need everyone in the world."

Sella ducked behind the counter, eyeing the ingredients that she had used. Something was amiss. There was no way her friend had drank cups of calming blend then decided to hop away outside on a clue hunt. She hated working in someone else's kitchen, with someone else's ingredients and recipes. It was part of the reason why she broke away from the company she had met Sediri at in the first place.

She grabbed one of the glass jars and popped back up, holding the powder to the light.

"Everything alright?" Verol asked, her mug hovering just before her lips.

Sella looked down at her with a smile she hoped didn't look too fake. "Yes," she said confidently. "The coffee is fine, I just think it won't be as calming as I had hoped."

"Calming coffee… Kind of an opposite, isn't it?"

Sella shrugged. She put the jar down but still eyed it suspiciously. "Perhaps," she said. "Not back home."

Verol hummed and then took another sip. "It feels soothing to me, for what it's worth. And that's an impressive feat considering… Well, everything."

A hint of pride bloomed in Sella's chest. She stuffed it down quickly. She needed to focus her energy where it mattered. "Baz has been here before, then?" Sella changed the subject.

Verol nodded. "Well, it's not right to keep you from an investigation, but I'm afraid I don't have much more information. He was generally despised and usually hateful. I think you'll be surprised to find that this small town has plenty of secrets of its own." She set her mug and a few coins down on the counter and gave Sella one curt nod before she exited the shop, leaving Sella all alone with her thoughts.

The Black Feather Potions & Pastries Detective Agency

The ~~Practical Potions~~
Black Feather Potions & Pastries
Detective Agency

EVERY SMALL TOWN that Sella had traveled to held the same few things, no matter how different they were from the outside. Nearly every town had a place to gather. A spot where most folks got together to gossip about the day, or even just sit in silence with others nearby, as though the mere presence of others was enough to soothe and recharge their hearts.

Sella couldn't relate. She needed to be up early most mornings and spent the evenings making pastries infused with compassion and patience, thinking of what the daily special ought to be based around what customers had said that day, or simply avoiding people so as not to catch the occasional overheard insult.

But there was something wonderful about the consistency of the gathering spot that did appeal to her, even though she was reluctant to admit it – even to herself.

Sunfall was no different. And she was glad for it. It was nice to know that despite a murder and despite being in a strange land where she didn't know the customs and stood out like a distant storm cloud on a clear day, the town was just like any other, when it really came down to it.

The tavern was smaller than the one in Marra, and much more dimly lit with a large fireplace in one corner and a few candles placed about the few tables. The candles were all old, dripping cream colored wax until it built up on the tabletops. Their flames flickered whenever someone walked past, and though they struggled against the dark, their light was still muted.

Sella looked up at the high ceiling, at the rafters that were so much lower than at Hazen's. The effect was like being in a cozy cave, though she was a little uneasy since she was used to feeling more expansive.

It was crowded tonight, though the two remaining soldiers were given such a wide radius in their corner that the space appeared fuller than it was. Everyone inside had gathered around the long bar opposite of the door, leaving the uniformed men to drink alone at their isolated table.

Sella's gaze lingered on them for a moment. She couldn't help but feel pity for them. It was clear that they weren't exactly welcome in town. And that perhaps now, more than ever, they were in need of a warm conversation. Still, she didn't feel bad enough to volunteer herself. The last thing her little group needed was to either draw attention to themselves or alienate themselves from the rest of the town.

Before they left their home, Beejee had warned her to keep her head down. And she knew he was right. She wanted to help. Some big part of her that grew with every passing moment with Cali did. But not at the detriment of her own safety or the safety of those she loved.

So for now, she, Lohrna, and Cali huddled at the end of the bar, watching Verol work and talk with the other villagers. Sella wasn't sure what she was looking for, exactly. She didn't know anyone. She didn't even know Verol. Not really.

Sella had only served up coffees and potions for a few days to a few people. She had no idea if anyone was acting strangely or what anyone's baseline of behavior was. She didn't know if anyone had any half-hidden grievance with Baz or was happy he was gone.

Sella was across the sea. And stuck.

Cali grasped at Sella's arm quickly. She gestured to the other end of the bar with an excitement on her face. "Verol's talking to some people," she whispered, as though she was trying to be sneaky despite no one else being able to hear her.

Sella's eyes flicked to Verol. She supposed it was true

that here, Verol could see and hear her. Perhaps many more could, too. Witches were more plentiful here. She tried not to stare as she watched Verol and the group of people she was talking to. What about their conversation was strange to Cali?

Sella shifted in her seat a little.

Verol's demeanor turned serious. She stood up straighter, then looked over at the military at the corner. Her eyes narrowed, and she ducked back down to speak to the group.

"What do you–?"

Cali grabbed Sella again. "She's coming this way," she said.

Verol was, and she was leading the group over with her. "Well, don't be so suspicious about it," Sella heard Verol whisper to the few humans.

Lohrna nearly leapt from her seat when the humans got close. She thrust her hand forward, palm up. "Hi," she said with all the energy Sella couldn't muster.

The humans took turns shaking her hand, though the first politely and subtly guided Lohrna's hand to the proper position. They seemed kind, at least they kindly helped with their traditions, but Sella wondered what would be suspicious.

Her friend didn't seem to have the same trepidation. "I'm Lohrna. This is Sella. Beejee, her talking cat is back at home, but I'm sure you've seen him around," she said brightly, a genuine smile taking up most of her face.

Sella felt her own forming on her lips. Her chest

expanded and she sat up straighter as a warm gratitude washed over her.

The people just stood there, awkwardly waiting but for what, Sella wasn't sure.

"Give them your short name," Verol said from behind the bar.

One of the man's eyes widened.

"Nothing nefarious," Verol explained as she reached down to get a fresh glass and a bundle of mushrooms, tied with a coarse-looking string. "Hear how short their names are? Just trust me, you don't want to stand here and listen to them fumble with the pronunciation." She smiled kindly. "Not to be rude," she added quickly. "But we just don't have the time for that now."

Lohrna nodded, her laugh bubbled up from her chest. Good natured as always. "That's true. It's really quite embarrassing. But we do mean well."

The human woman who, at first, seemed concerned about the two strangers with horns, now relaxed her stance. She gathered her long black hair, worn down in braids, and moved it over one shoulder. Earrings decorated every part of her ear, shimmering in the candle light.

Sella recognized her as the woman who had confronted the wyvern riders. Her brows lifted slightly, surprised that she seemed a bit nervous now but had no fear when she spoke to the military riding huge monsters.

"You can call me Rae," the woman said at last.

"Call me Echori," the smaller man beside her said.

He looked from Lohrna to Sella. "So which one of you is the kitchen witch?"

Sella raised her hand. Beside her, Cali shimmered out of view. "Be careful," Sella wanted to say, but she stayed quiet instead. Cali knew what she was doing.

"I'm sorry we haven't been able to visit your shop yet," Rae said.

"It's not really mine," Sella explained. "We're setting it up for Sediri, a witch from our home island. We're helping to set things up, get the business launched, while she is away. She should be back soon, though."

Rae cocked her head. "Is that so? The red haired one?"

Lohrna nodded. "That's her!"

"She has worked her whole career at a shop with strict regulations," Sella explained. "Now that she has freedom, it's a bit difficult."

Echori took a long drink. "I see," he said. "So she needs someone who can run the business side of things?"

"For a bit," Sella said. "We have a ticket back home already purchased."

"Though maybe we'll stay a little longer?" Lohrna suggested in a sing-song tune, like a child suggesting something they knew they shouldn't. "You know, since we can help out with the investigation. If you're worried about it, don't be. We're on the case!"

Sella glared at her, for just a moment. Her heart quickened. "We're not making any promises—"

"In addition to being a *certified* kitchen witch back home, Sella and I, and Cali, have opened up the Practical

Potions Detective Agency! We're consultants. Have the paperwork and everything," Lohrna cut her off.

Echori and Rae exchanged quick looks. They seemed amused. Or relieved. It was hard to tell.

Verol, still busy slicing the small capped mushrooms, smiled. "See?" she said with a grin, "I told you we'd be fine. I trust them." She glanced back to the corner of the tavern, then ducked her head a little, making herself look concentrated on her work. She added in a whisper, "Besides, the death of Baz has nothing to do with any of us. Whoever did it had their list. And we're not on it."

Rae looked down at the floor with narrowed eyes. She shook her head a little. "Nothing good can come of this. It doesn't quite matter why they did it, or if they aren't a danger to anyone else. We still need to find whoever did this."

Lohrna ducked to catch her stare, she was bright as always. "Don't worry," she said. "We can handle this."

Sella wished that, like a ghost, she could simply disappear. She didn't think they could handle this at all. In fact, it was so much bigger than anything else they had ever faced.

"Thank you," Rae said at last.

Oh, tides low and high… Beejee was going to hate this.

TEN

Interview with a Wyvern

"Since when do you care about helping Sediri out?" Lohrna said. Her arms were crossed over her chest, her stare teasing.

They stood in the shop, just beside the door, with Beejee standing firmly between them, blocking the way out. He was puffing himself up, ready, it seemed, to scratch at anyone who dared move him.

Sella wondered for a moment if she should remind Lohrna that, as a familiar, he did possess magic and could use it, if he needed to. He looked like he might try.

"We get a cut of the profits, too while she's away," Beejee said. "I'm not missing out on humans buying up luck and calm and safety with a murderer in town."

Sella shrugged. "I mean, I'm still working on the signature luck blend," she said.

"Not the point," Beejee said.

Cali bent down slowly, making herself small at his level. "Beejee," she said quietly. "We can all go see what we can find out, or it can just be me and you out there. I need someone to speak for me."

Beejee thrust his head up. "Fine. Then Sella can run the shop here and we'll go do it."

Cali giggled. "Alright. So you're fine with explaining to everyone we talk to, every time, that you're a familiar, with a special spell to speak, talking for a ghost of a human who traveled across the sea with the witch and a shifter—"

Beejee hissed. He stomped one little paw down. "You're impossible!"

Cali looked up at Sella with a smile and wink.

Warmth spread through Sella's body. The tips of her ears reddened.

"So, is that a yes, you'll let us through?" Lohrna asked. "Come on, Beejee. It'll be like the old days of solving mysteries together. It'll be fun."

"Why can't Sella and I stay to run the place?" Beejee gave it one final point.

Sella crossed her arms. "Beejee, they need us. There's giant wyverns out there."

Beejee, very slowly, moved aside.

Lohrna pumped a fist in the air. "Alright! Let's go look for clues!" She opened the door and bright yellow light filled the room. A wave of hot air hit their bodies as they filed out into the morning air.

"You know… in these good old days you speak of, you got arrested for murder," Beejee grumbled.

Lohrna waved a hand dismissively. "Oh, that was a decoy. Benka knew what he was doing."

Sella sighed. That time in her life had been harrowing. At least, for a few moments there. Lohrna had, in fact, been publicly arrested for Cali's murder and spent a night in jail. Though, the ancient detective in town had done so to push Sella into finishing the investigation. It still was a memory that filled her with a sense of dread, even years later. "Can we move on to the present moment, please?" she asked.

Cali's hand found Sella's. She squeezed it and rested her head on Sella's shoulder as they walked down the street toward the market. "I think this whole thing is kind of exciting. In a strange way," she said. "It does force you out of the shop."

Sella had to admire her optimism. It was true, she'd probably be relegated to the shop most of the time, either by her own anxiety, or Beejee's insistence that they use this opportunity to build up a decent savings. But now, here they were, on their way to the early morning market and–

As they turned the corner, they ran directly into a wyvern.

Lohrna let out a loud gasp, she jumped back, her hands up.

Sella's palms ignited with fire, burning brightly in the sunlight.

At her side, Cali's arm turned solid, moving to block Sella from taking one more step. She looked down at Sella's hands and shook her head.

Sella's heart was pounding in her chest, her fire ready. She took a deep breath in and held it until it hurt. Her fire extinguished, and the beast before them blinked slowly.

The wyvern, though easily three times taller than any human, was shockingly good at hiding among the two story, sand colored buildings. Its head was low. Its long, scaled neck bent down to meet their eyes with its own amber stare.

It turned a little, moving so one eye could get a better look at the group, so close that Sella could see their reflections staring back at themselves in its iris.

Sella wasn't sure what Cali thought she could do with her arm out to defend them, but she knew enough to understand that it meant they should be still for the moment.

She studied the massive face before them, eyes following the curve of its horns, the detail of its dark blue-green scales as they rippled over the thick muscle in its jaw. A few pointed teeth jutted out from its upper lip.

It blinked, then snorted through a slitted nostril, seemingly content to not do any damage to them. Though it looked like it would be very, very easy for it to try.

"Lucanairi!" A strong voice called from behind the wyvern.

It shook its head, then whipped its neck back, standing taller on its thick legs. It extended its leather wings just a little. The posture looked like a sign of annoyance. Sella was familiar with her own familiar's attitude enough to tell.

She tucked her hands into her pockets quickly. She found the stick, her fake wand, and gripped it tightly.

Two men, their uniforms disheveled and wrinkled, appeared from behind the wyvern. They looked just as shocked as Sella to see the group standing there.

"Ah," the taller man said. "Sorry about Lucanairi." He hurried to the wyvern's side and put a hand on its neck with a gentle touch. "He won't strike without command, I can assure you."

Sella's eyes narrowed. She felt Beejee's soft fur on her calf. "You can assure that?" she asked.

Cali's hand moved to wrap around Sella protectively. She widened her stance. "It depends on the wyvern," Cali said, her voice so confident and calm, Sella looked at the humans, wondering if they had been able to hear her, even a little. "This one is misbehaved. I don't know if they have total control over it."

Lohrna, however, seemingly over her initial fear, stepped closer to the large creature. "It's beautiful…" she whispered at last.

The shorter of the two, a stocky man with a bald head and a gentle expression, laughed. His eyes lingered on Lohrna's horns. "Never seen one up close?"

"Never seen one at all," Lohrna said. "We're from Orakan."

"I can see that," he said, though not unkindly. There was a warmth to his tone. But it made Sella all the more unsure about him.

The wyvern shook its head again, then pressed its snout up to the taller man.

"Excuse him," the taller of the two said. "It's close to

feeding time and… Well, with his rider gone… he is just a little lost right now.”

Cali's fingers pressed into Sella's side. She looked up at her and smiled, though it didn't reach her eyes. “We should go with them, pretend to be interested in the novelty of it but we can get information out of them,” she said.

Beejee meowed. Loudly. An agreement, though clearly he didn't want to reveal that he could speak just yet.

Sella took a long breath in. It would be easy to get Lohrna excitedly asking questions. She cast her friend a quick look and summoned her courage as best she could. “It's feeding time?” Sella said, hoping her excitement didn't sound too fake. “May we come along?”

“Oh! Yes please!” Lohrna's enthusiasm was infectious.

Sella watched as the soldiers' postures softened at her glee.

“I'm Lohrna. This is Sella. And Beejee!”

Sella could sense Cali's unease at her side begin to dissipate, her hand relaxed to an easy position on Sella's waist.

“Motetzelial,” the taller soldier said. His name, Sella assumed. He gestured to the shorter, older man. “This is Tateliali.”

“I'll do my best to remember that,” Lohrna said, social as always. “So, we're coming, right? What do wyverns eat? Is it gnarly?”

Tateliali laughed and the wyvern snapped at the air beside him. “It's not always for the gentle,” he said.

"What do you say, Motetzelial? Should we show the little villagers?"

Motetzeilal cocked his head. He was studying Sella with the same look she was sure she had been giving him. Half curious, half suspicious. She wasn't sure which side was winning until his eyes widened a little and the corners of his lips turned up. "Why not?" he said at last. He turned and waved for the wyvern to follow.

On feet curiously silent for its size, the wyvern shifted and moved down the alleyway with swift ease.

Cali bent down to Beejee. "Let's do this!"

Beejee meowed back and the group followed the soldiers through the streets. It didn't take long to make their way to the edge of the town, surrounded by open fields of sharp studded plants and dry, empty land.

A single structure stood at the perimeter of the town.

It was a large barn, big enough to easily fit the three wyverns, and more. It was made of sun-bleached wood, splintered in a few places from the heat, and covered in scratches, Sella assumed, from the wyverns. It looked exotic among the clay texture that most of the town was built in. It was well kept, though, with a big flat roof made of a silver metal showing no signs of rust or damage.

A bead of sweat ran down Sella's neck. Her arms tingled with a creeping sense of dread, remembering that there were two more wyverns, most likely inside. Her hands curled into loose fists at her sides. She tried thinking of a question to ask, something innocent sounding… "Is this where you're staying?"

Tateliali chuckled, a surprisingly light sound. "Oh no. This is where the wyverns stay. We're not beasts."

Beejee's eyes narrowed at him, but he kept his opinion to himself.

For now.

Sella was certain she'd be hearing him rant about it later.

"Come on, we'll show you how it's done," Tateilali said with a nod of his head for them to follow.

"Exciting!" There was a skip to Lohrna's steps as she followed along. Sella was sure her excitement was genuine. But her next question made Sella smile. "So, anything to be worried about? Wyvern's breathe fire, don't they? I don't want to end up like that one guy."

Motetzeilal opened the door to the barn with a low grunt, straining against the door that didn't want to be moved. "They don't," he said over his shoulder. "Most don't."

Lucanairi moved inside the barn with an almost chirp-like sound, swallowed up into the darkness as quickly as he had arrived.

Lohrna squinted into the dark of the barn. She leaned forward. "Right... Sorry, I don't mean to sound insensitive."

Tateliali and Motetzeilal exchanged a quick look.

Tides. They must not have been as subtle as they had hoped.

"You're the Wyldes... with the detective agency back home?" Motetzeilal said as he slipped inside the shadows.

Sella wasn't sure how they found out and it made her

anxious, but Lohrna seemed to take it in stride. She held up her hands, she was smiling; caught in the lie. "Guilty," she said with a laugh. "*But*, I really do want to see the wyverns and learn about them. We have a human friend who told us all about them. I've been fascinated ever since. Truce?"

Tateliali followed his fellow soldier. "Come on," he said. "I think we ought to reward curiosity more often. It's a lost trait these days."

Lohrna looked back at Sella, crinkles forming at the corners of her eyes. She pumped one fist silently, then slipped inside behind the two men.

Beejee's fur was puffed between his shoulderblades. "Stay close," he warned, his voice so low Sella's wasn't sure if he had truly said it aloud.

Beside her, Cali's form grew more opaque. She set her jaw and followed Lohrna. "Stay close."

The corners of Sella's mouth twitched, despite the coursing anxiety flowing through her bloodstream. What were a cat and ghost going to do to protect her? Even if they were a magic wielding cat and an unusually strong ghost.

Still, their courage led her in.

As her eyes adjusted to the sudden darkness, she made out the three large figures, nestled together along the far wall.

"If you want to know about the wyverns, we can tell you. And if you want to know what we know about the murder, we can tell you that too," Tateliali said from a corner of the barn.

"Baziliari and I got into a hot talk the night he died," Motetzeilal said, following his partner's lead. His voice was confident as he picked up a large wooden bucket. He held it close to his chest and stared at Sella with eyes growing more intense as her own adjusted to the darkness.

'Hot talk?' It sounded like 'an argument', but if it meant a lesser version, like a mild disagreement, or something more fierce, she wasn't sure. She'd have to check in with Cali later.

"I won't discuss the details of the conversation. They're not relevant nor are they for me to say. We were in the forge," the soldier went on. "I turned to leave, and heard a powerful sound. A fire erupted. And just like that, he was gone." He moved to the edge of the barn, and cast the bucket down before the wyverns.

Each of their long, scaled necks arched down in sweeping motions and their jaws began to snap wildly at the floor.

Lohrna's gaze fell on Sella quickly, then shifted away to the wyverns.

Motetzeilal backed up slowly until he stood beside Tateliali. Both watched the wyverns, their heads moving with each wyvern to make sure they were all eating.

Lucanairi moved his head around the others, nudging the smallest wyvern gently when it strayed too far from the center.

Tateliali reached up, placing a hand gently on Motetzeilal's shoulder.

Motetzelial went on, "My wyvern doesn't breathe fire.

Tateliali's doesn't either." He looked at Sella. "I'm guilty of a lot of things. But not mutiny."

Tateliali cocked his head to Lohrna. "Baz was not a good leader. But we follow orders. Besides, if you want to learn about wyverns– know this, they can't breathe fire if they don't naturally have the ability. And they can't without the permission of their bonded rider. In the wild, what few there are left, there is no documented account of a wyvern using fire."

Cali crossed her arms over her chest. "He's right," she said. "We don't have magic, not like witches. But the military here are different. It's why my whole family joined. Why they cut me off when I didn't." Her voice cracked at the end. She looked away. "Wyverns need a strong bond to breath fire, and most still can't even with the strong connection."

Sella reached out to her. She didn't care that the soldiers couldn't see why. Cali leaned into Sella's shoulder.

The sound of the wyverns' jaws crunched in the air, drowning out Sella's thoughts.

"What do you mean they can't without permission?" Lohrna asked, seemingly as both a deflection from Sella and true curiosity.

Tateliali lowered his hand at last. "Come with me," he said. He gestured for Lohrna to follow.

Lohrna did, easing closer slowly behind him toward the wyverns.

Sella's body stiffened. Her hands grew warm as Cali slipped from her embrace. She stepped closer to Lohrna, ready to burn anything that sprung at her.

Tateliali's expression was kind, unaware of the danger lurking behind him. He pointed to the bucket as they all grew closer.

"Bugs?" Lohrna gasped. "They eat *bugs?*"

Tateliali laughed. "Everyone's always surprised. In the wild, they hunt bigger game. But we can't have any more bad rumors about them by having them destroy the local ecosystems. Insects work well and it keeps their hunting instincts in check." He stayed quiet for a long moment as the wyverns finished their meals. One of the larger ones licked its lips, seemingly satisfied with their lunch. Tateliali went on, "Motetzelial has been open about his disagreements with command. He's right, though. Even if he wanted to harm Baziliari with Lucanairi's fire, he couldn't. Wyverns and their riders have a profound bond. No one else would be able to give the command. It wasn't Lucanairi that did this."

One of them, a red-hued wyvern, shook its head out, a layer of fine sand dusting around its body like a halo of gold as it did.

"If a wyvern can breathe fire, it is only through the help of its rider. Think of the beast as emotion. The human as reason. Fire, the emotion can spring forth. But logic needs to direct it." He turned back to his friend. "Unfortunately, detectives, this lead has led you to the edge of the canyon."

ELEVEN

That One Time Baz Burned Down a Barn

"END OF THE SHORE, my full moon!" Lohrna whispered when the group was finally out of sight of the barn.

"I think the phrase was 'end of the canyon'?" Sella said with a small shrug.

Beejee trotted quickly beside her. "I agree with Lohrna. They seem suspicious."

"But you're suspicious of everyone, Beejee," Cali said, her voice was kind, though she giggled a little, clearly teasing him.

Sella bit the inside of her lip gently. She turned over the soldiers' words in her mind, smoothing them like riverrock. "I think I'm inclined to believe them," she said at last.

They had found their way back into the little village, surrounded by the big clay buildings, with all their little windows shut tight with colorful wood panels. She looked up, the sun was in the middle of the clear cyan sky.

It was midday. The people here closed shops and either rested, or went to the Verol's around this time.

Good. She didn't want to interact with anyone else.

She cast a glance at Lohrna and Beejee who both looked at her with narrowed eyes. Lohrna's, at least, seemed like an insincere annoyance whereas Beejee was downright frustrated. "Wyvern's can't breathe fire without their humans," Sella said with another shrug. "It sounds like the only wyvern who can even *with* one was Baz's."

Lohrna shook her head. "Yes, but isn't it most likely that it was wyvern fire that burnt the guy? I mean, Sella, otherwise, it's an elemental witch. And that…"

"Would be catastrophic," Beejee finished for her.

"Maybe something in the forge was faulty and it… I don't know… exploded?" Cali suggested.

Beejee looked up at her and spat, a little sound of disgust at the idea. "The forge wouldn't just explode on one person and nothing else. It was contained enough that the fire was directed."

They turned the corner and into the large square where all the little booths were closed, covered with colorful heavy rugs to keep the various wares safe from the heat of the sun.

Sella paused. She let out a quick breath, then crossed one arm around her stomach. "Let's get something to eat," she said. "We can ask around at the tavern. See if we can learn more about Baz."

"And then we stowaway on the next boat," Beejee grumbled.

Sella shook her head. "We made a promise to Sediri.

And… it's just not time to leave yet." Her eyes flicked to Cali at her side. She had made a promise to her, too. There were more witches here, kinds of magic she didn't know. She was going to find a spell to help Cali.

And it wasn't in Orakan.

"Come on," Sella said. "We can figure this out."

"Where's this confidence coming from?" Beejee grumbled. Though, as Sella's chest expanded, she knew she felt his pride swell through her.

SELLA SWIRLED the wine in her cup, watching her own blurry reflection in its red shimmer. She missed Hazen. His happy laugh and stern disposition. She missed her bees. Missed the honey flavors from home. She wished she could close her eyes, take a deep breath, and magic her way back. Even just for the afternoon.

Cali's cold hand crept up her arm like a fog. "I miss the rain, too," she said softly.

Sella's face softened. She smiled at Cali, though she felt the worry lines between her brows deepen. She didn't want Cali thinking she didn't enjoy being in her homeland, but it was hard to hide her discomfort. She decided to stay quiet, and simply take a long sip of her wine.

The tavern was less busy than Sella would have expected. They sat at the counter beside Echori and Rae, the two humans they had met before who seemed like they were here often, and, thankfully, knew a lot about the town and its people, judging by their keen stares and occasional commentary about whoever happened to walk in after them.

Sella was glad to see somewhat familiar faces, at least.

Beside her, Lohrna was gesturing wildly at Verol. "They eat *bugs*!" Lohrna's voice pulled Sella back from the depths. "Lots and lots of bugs."

Verol raised a brow, she was busy pouring another drink behind the counter. "Live ones?"

Lohrna sat back. "You know, that's a good question. I didn't get that close."

Verol laughed, a light sound like the wind chimes they heard out in the market. "I don't blame you," she said.

"I'm surprised they care about their reputation. Baziliari was always using his wyvern as a sword and a shield. Throwing that scaled beast's might around like it was his own to wield. I have a hard time believing that the military tries to temper down their wyverns' instincts," Echori said. He leaned in a little to catch Sella's faraway gaze. "You're a witch. Do you see anything about this whole thing?"

Verol rolled her eyes. "Don't be like that, Echori. You know she's a kitchen witch."

"Still can have the sight," Echori said with a shrug.

Sella cocked her head. "The sight?"

Verol nodded with a warm grin. "You don't have fortune tellers on your island?"

Sella sank lower in her seat.

Lohrna spoke for her, "Orakan has really more of a kitchen witch focus. It's funny, back home we have all these things you might consider magic but... the witches are a different story." She rubbed her friend's back with one hand, then slapped it, a little too hard.

Sella coughed.

"But, she is certified!" Lohrna said, ignoring her. "That's how she met Sediri, right? Working in a shop?"

Sella nodded. Close enough.

Rae slid her cup across the bar for Verol to refill.

Verol poured something iced and bright into her mug. "It's crushed ice, with silktop mushrooms mixed in," Verol explained as Lohrna leaned in for a better look. "I'll pour you some next round. It will keep your body moving well in the heat. No magic, just good nutrition."

"I'll take one now," Lohrna said, downing her own drink quickly. She slid her cup to Verol, then turned back to the humans beside her. "Well, why don't we find a fortune teller witch. Do you have any in town? That would help a lot with our investigation to have someone with *the sight*, wouldn't it?"

Rae tossed a braid over her shoulder. "Oh, I'm sure you'll find the culprit without one."

"Besides the fact that they can only see very specific things," Verol mumbled.

"And we don't have one in town." Rae went on, her intensity grew as she spoke, "Baziliari had enemies. Now, which ones could hurt him like that, I'm not sure. But he did not make friends easily. He burned down the barn just outside of town not too many years ago. I don't even remember what the offense was."

Cali pushed herself up onto the bar. Her legs dangled over the side, swinging carefree. "That makes sense," she said. "Even his own in his ranks didn't seem to enjoy him. They weren't sad about his death, and openly admitted to having a heated disagreement just before he died. Like it was commonplace."

Sella tilted her cup to Cali. She had a point. Still, justice was justice. He didn't deserve to die just because a lot of people wanted him dead. Though, she was sure Beejee might disagree. Especially now that it was creating more work for them.

For now, her familiar remained at the other side of the tavern, slipping through tables and chairs, his ear flicking when he picked up a bit of conversation he thought was noteworthy.

"But wait, sure he wasn't popular, but… Who owned the barn? That sounds like one big lead. Plus, it's poetry isn't it? Burn a burn, get burned?" Lohrna asked.

Verol looked away. "I did," she whispered. "But, no, I didn't kill him."

Lohrna's eyes widened. "It was *your* barn? What happened?"

Verol sighed and glanced up at the ceiling. "It belonged to my family for a long time," she said, busying herself with rearranging something behind the counter that they could not see. Glass bottles clanked together, muddying her voice. "Years ago, he and his soldiers came here. It was a stop on the way to someplace else. And. They were a different set under his command. I don't even know these soldiers."

Lohrna's brows knit together. She tilted her body

closer. "It's alright," she whispered softly. "You can tell us."

Verol blinked a few times. She went back to moving items under the bar and when we spoke again, her voice was hoarse. "He wanted to store his wyverns there. At my family's barn. I said no, it housed many of my plants that cannot be exposed to the direct sunlight here. They're fragile and I need them for my work. So…" Verol's gaze met Sella's. Her jaw was set tight, her expression burrowing into the other witch as if she was trying to tell her something without speaking. Verol went on, "He burned it down."

Sella's eyes searched Verol's, but she couldn't find anything but a wall between them.

"What happened?" Lohrna said.

Verol sighed, then covered it with a fake smile. "I never said no again."

TWELVE

Scones, Finally

IN THE FLICKERING light of little floating fires overhead, the group of Wyldes gathered around the couch and low table, each with their own mug beside them. The smell of clove and spice warmed the space around them as trails of steam rose from the dark green liquid. Sella had added a little clarity to the cups, the hint of earth mixing in subtly at the finish.

Lohrna lay on her stomach, kicking her feet in the air lazily and resting her head in the crook of her elbow on the floor. The tip of one antler grazed a deep groove in the wood and she watched the steam rise higher in the air, following it until it disappeared into the dark.

Beejee sat beside her. His tail thumped dully in a heartbeat rhythm.

Sella's legs rested on the couch, though her back was flat against the floor. She stared at the ceiling, watching her fires float by slowly, and feeling very old. Her back hurt. Her feet hurt. She was thirsty. And she didn't really want to do anything about any of it. She closed her eyes for a long while until she heard Cali's voice close.

"What are we doing?" Cali asked. Excitement filled the air like a spark, so bright, she even felt Lohrna flinch beside her.

Sella opened one eye. "Trying to figure out where to go next," she said, hopeful that it would sound like she was ready to do *something* when the reality was, she was more shaken by Verol's news than she expected to be. All she really wanted was to drift away and float home.

Cali hovered over Sella's face with a gentle smile. She placed two cold hands on either side of Sella's forehead and held her steady. "Well, how about we don't think about that right now." She leaned down, her lips kissed Sella's brow, nearly solid. "Let's just have some fun for a moment."

Beejee let out a little grunt.

"Come on, sit up." Cali nudged Sella's head.

Sella let out a little moan and rose up onto her elbows.

"Get Lohrna up too," Cali nearly ordered. "I'm going to teach you both some more human customs so you don't make fools of yourselves when there's an open investigation."

"Now you're teaching us?" Sella asked. They had been in Tollintal for days.

"Well, the best teacher is experience," Cali said with a laugh. "The second best is under threat of arrest." She turned and poked Lohrna with her foot.

Lohrna turned toward Cali. "Cal?"

Sella finally rose to a sitting position on the floor, her back leaning up against the couch. "Cali is going to teach us some human customs so we don't make ourselves look suspicious," Sella explained.

"More suspicious," Beejee corrected with his eyes still closed.

Lohrna scrambled up. "Let's do it!" She looked in the direction where Cali had touched her, though the ghost was already sitting across from her. "What's the deal with the thing where they put their hand up and on their heart? Is that like a ritual?"

Cali laughed. "I'll explain everything. But a lot of it still won't make sense. Most of it doesn't for me either."

Sella rolled her neck slowly, summoning the strength to stand. They had a business to run, despite everything. And she had work to do. She needed to keep trying to make the lucky blend, and make scones for the morning. "Can you translate, Beejee?" Sella asked as she finally rose from her seat. Her legs tingled at the sudden movement but she grabbed her clarity tea and sipped it slowly anyway.

Beejee ignored her but his ear flicked. A sure sign he had heard her.

"Where are you going?" Both Cali and Lohrna asked.

"Just do some baking for tomorrow," Sella said gently. She crossed the room to the little kitchen where a wood-fire oven was built into the wall. It was small, much smaller than the one she had at home. She suspected that the people of Sunfall probably didn't do much warm cooking for most of the year. Still, it meant she had to make extra batches to produce the same amount.

She tapped her cheek slowly, trying to think of what to make the people here as she listened to Beejee, despite everything, enthusiastically translate the customs of Tollintal to Lohrna.

He, of course, wasted no chance to correct Lohrna's movements with his little paw.

Sella got to work preparing her ingredients and with a flick of her wrist, the oven lit and the room was filled with warmth, and laughter, and the smell of fresh lemon, bright and fragrant in the calm one room flat.

WHEN THEY WERE READY, Sella finished the scones with a sprinkle of crystal sugar that shimmered like little jewels in the firelight.

Lohrna had long been asleep at the foot of the bed, one arm tossed over her eyes and her mouth hung open, with little snores escaping her throat from time to time. Beejee curled up next to her, his fur rising and falling slowly as he slumbered deeply in her warmth.

Cali was sitting up at the counter, watching Sella work. She sniffed the air and smiled. "Forget a spell to speak," she said. "I want a spell to eat."

Sella looked up at her. "Now you tell me," she teased.

Cali hopped off the counter with a strange lightness, as though she hovered just a little too long in the air. When she touched the ground again, she bounded to

Sella and wrapped her arms around her waist. She looked up at the witch with a playful expression.

Warmth burned through Sella's limbs and into her chest. She smiled down at Cali and pressed her forehead to the ghost's.

"You don't need to be worried," Cali whispered. "What was it Seaglass said? 'Worry is just your mind trying to predict the future'?"

Sella pulled Cali in closer. She took in a long breath. "Something like that," she said. Seaglass, the mythical sea creature she went to when things were at their absolute worst, had a habit of speaking in riddles and half puzzles, and in a way that made Sella want to scream. But hearing it through Cali somehow softened the sting of frustration.

They were right. And Sella knew it.

There was no sense in worrying about what tomorrow was going to bring because the future was uncertain and random.

A part of Sella, the part that never thought she'd find herself here, in the arms of a ghost on a continent away from home, was glad for it. She could never have imagined life becoming so beautiful and strange.

Perhaps tomorrow would bring something just as lovely.

Sella nodded and felt herself begin to sway.

Cali smiled, and the two danced gently in the small kitchen while the rest of the town slept.

THIRTEEN

Cats and Catastrophizing

THE SHOP HAD BEEN open for business since dawn, but Sella had been too busy working on potions in the back to notice that the sun had climbed higher into the sky and no one had shown up yet.

Beejee, however, paced in front of the door, his ear flicking every so often with frustration. "You know, if I were a villager, I'd be banging down this door to get my hands on a luck spell, or a protection charm," he grumbled. "What is wrong with everyone?"

Sella looked up from her stone mortar, pestle still crushing the herbs gently. "Yes, well the luck spell is still a work in progress."

"*They* don't know that." He trotted across the shop, leaped up onto the counter, and thrust his nose toward the fragrant herbs. "How is it going, by the way…?"

Sella shrugged.

"Sediri doesn't deserve all this attention for a signature spell she's not even helping create," Beejee said at last. He sat up straight, attention back to the door.

"I agree," Sella said. "But, on the other side, it would be nice to have a little luck come our way for once. I still need to fix the wand, and find a spell to help Cali…"

Beejee nodded. "This is true."

"So, I'll keep working at it," she said. "If that's fine with you."

Her familiar purred in return just as the shop door opened slowly and a little white cat scampered in with Verol close behind.

"Glad to see you're open," Verol said with a warm smile. She shut the door behind her gently and cast a long glance out the window.

Sella's jaw tightened, just for a moment. She did her best to put on her customer service smile, though she still squared her shoulders as Verol crossed the shop. "Every-thing alright?"

Verol's brows rose. "Of course," she said. "Just the storms might be rolling in soon."

"Storms?" Beejee asked before Sella could.

Verol nodded. "They happen every year in these parts. Didn't Cali tell you?"

Cali appeared by Sella, a flash of sudden color. "I didn't really think about it," she said, a bit defensively as if she had just been mildly insulted. "We don't have them in the big cities."

Verol smiled. "Of course," she said. "Bigger witch population, better control of such things."

Cali shrugged, her shoulder brushing Sella's as she stood closer. "We have a development," she whispered.

"That's actually what I came to tell you about," Verol said. She leaned across the counter and her fingers tapped gently on the wood as if she was trying to muddle her voice. "The military has brought in a detective to handle the case."

Sella looked at Cali, then Verol.

She had stopped tapping, but now her fingers were tightly laced together, bones paling her skin as she held firm.

"This isn't a good thing, then?" Sella pushed her ingredients to the side carefully.

Verol shook her head. "I'm guessing they'll want this thing solved quickly. And quickly doesn't always mean accurately."

A small breeze blew through the room and Verol shivered. Cali's hair shifted around her elbows. She was upset.

"We don't know that," Cali said sternly. She lifted her chin defiantly and placed a solid hand on Sella's shoulder. "No need to catastrophize right now."

Sella wrapped one arm around her core. Cali was trying to protect her, to keep her mind from spiraling as it so often did with bad news.

It wasn't fair to her and she felt acidity rise up in her stomach at the thought of Cali wasting any more time worrying about her. She took in a long breath and stood taller. "We'll handle it," she said, trying to sound as confident as she could.

"The military isn't known for getting along with witches," Verol said.

"Not historically," Cali corrected. "We don't know how this will go. We're a detective consultant agency back home. We'll work with the detective here, too. If we're helpful, it will go in our favor and we can keep the investigation on the right course."

Verol's familiar scratched at her long skirt, meowing. She glanced down, her expression softened.

Beejee's front paws extended. He stretched across the counter, nonchalant. "Let's close the shop for now," he said casually. "We'll go see this detective and offer up our services."

"For a fee?" Cali giggled. Her hand passed through Sella like smoke as she flickered, just a little. Her smile was practiced, not quite reaching her eyes.

"That was implied," Beejee said, already strutting for the door. "Don't be crude by saying it aloud."

"I can stay to run things here, if you need," Verol said. She pushed herself up from the counter, her fingers following the groove in the wood as if she couldn't quite compel herself to let go. "I'm not a kitchen witch, but I know herbs. I can help."

Sella shook her head, though she wasn't really sure why. Something about the way Verol lingered gave Sella pause. She explained, "Lohrna will be up soon. She'll handle it. You should rest. Get ready for the storm, or tonight…"

Beejee turned his head over his shoulder, his ear twitched.

"Alright," Verol said.

"If there's a storm coming, you should be somewhere safe," Beejee said to Verol's familiar. "Go back to the tavern with your witch."

Verol blinked a few times and finally lifted her hands, shoving them into her pockets. "I'll open up the tavern early I guess," she said. "Let me know if I can help, though."

They exited the shop together after Sella wrote a little note for Lohrna, but Verol turned right and the others turned left.

"Well, that wasn't at all suspicious," Beejee said as they walked down the road.

Cali leaned closer. "I agree," she said. "But there's a big part of me that doesn't want to give her any more trouble. She sounds like Baz has caused enough of that around here. Besides, she's kind and seems like she's doing her best around here…" She trailed off, looking back over her shoulder as if she was worried that the other witch might hear her, though she had long left their line of sight.

Beejee snorted through his little pink nose and Sella's stomach turned.

They were both right. And that was the worst part. Verol could be suspicious and have motive, and also be kind and helpful and in need of rest. It stung her chest to think too hard about it for now.

Cali's green eyes sparkled as she glanced at Sella. Her smile, genuine, widened. "We'll have more information soon enough, I'm sure of it." She pointed down the road to a little shop with its red wood shades flung open. "I saw him here," she said as they stopped in front of the clay building.

It was smaller than the other buildings along the street, narrow and only one level. The red lettering above the bright blue door read something that Sella didn't understand, though if it was because of the sun-bleached, peeling letters, or that it was a word she genuinely did not know, she couldn't be sure.

She tucked a lock of dark hair behind her pointed ear.

"Come on, we're looking like we're going to rob the place by just standing here," Beejee said as he nudged Sella's calf along with his forehead. He looked up at the sky.

Sella followed his gaze to the thick clouds beginning to encroach upon them. They were dark, heavy looking, but still so high above them. It was so unlike her home where it was always a pale gray overcast with low clouds holding the earth like a blanket. She furrowed her brow and followed behind Cali's disappearing form through the blue door.

A cluster of bells above the door chimed as they entered and a few humans turned toward them with fiery expressions as though Sella and Beejee had just disrupted something deeply important and highly secret.

Sella recognized a few faces, but the woman behind the counter with a close shaved head and brilliantly warm smile was new. As was the tall man who stood in the middle of the group.

The woman waved, almost too enthusiastically. "Welcome in!" she called, her voice as bold and bright as the bells in her shop.

Sella glanced around them, it was full, from the floor to ceiling with books. And while most were stacked neatly in the teal bookcases that lined each wall, many were placed haphazardly in piles along the floor and atop the one small table in the middle of the room.

The group of people smiled kindly, some raised a hand to Sella and Beejee in greeting before they whispered a quick parting to the woman behind the counter. They took turns shaking hands with the man in the middle, then moved their way past the stacks of books and Sella and back out of the shop.

Cali's voice whispered near Sella, "That's the detective. Don't look suspicious."

Sella's eyes shifted to the space where Cali's voice had been. But why wasn't she manifesting here… Sella stuffed a hand into her pocket and touched the stick that she had hidden there. The fake wand was still intact. Thank the tides.

Beejee stayed by her side, he looked up at her hand and then to the woman behind the counter.

She was a witch.

"I've been meaning to come in and say hello," the other witch said warmly. She urged them closer. "You're the new kitchen witch, right?"

"Substituting for the real one," Sella said. She hoped it came out kind but her heart beat faster in her chest, and she was worried everyone in the room could hear it.

She did her best to recover with a smile. "We're helping her set up here for now."

The man's eyes had not moved once from Sella since they came in. He was older, judging by his graying mustache and deep wrinkles on his forehead. He was dressed well, long and loose white pants and a structured pink shirt that climbed up his throat. It was the kind of fashion Sella had never seen, but it did look well made and of high quality.

Sella and Beejee walked closer to the counter and the man's eyes tracked their every step as though he was waiting to find a moment to strike. Her steps were light, her fingers still clutching the fake wand in her pocket as she fished the other out to extend to the detective. "I'm Sella," she said as confidently as she could. "This is Beejee."

The detective took her hand, gave it two firm shakes, and then he smiled. "Good to meet you, Sella, and Beejee. You can call me Poem." He let go of her hand and his attention shifted to Beejee. "Glad to see a familiar like you," he said.

Sella's lips tightened before she caught herself. She did her best to pretend she wasn't bothered by adjusting her hair behind her ear. What did he mean by that?

The woman behind the counter laughed as a black creature circled up and over her shoulder. It was long, like a snake, but covered in thick fur, and, as far as Sella could tell, seemed to have more than four legs with little paws that clung to the witch's loose overshirt. It looked at them with three bright blue eyes and chirped.

"My familiar is… unfamiliar, at least to the people here," she explained with a little shrug. She leaned her body over the counter and reached her arm long for Sella to grab.

Cautiously, Sella took her hand.

"I'm Lazil, and I'm not from here either," the witch said. She let go of Sella and turned back to the detective. "I was just telling Poem that I moved here a few years ago. I'm from the north. We have these little fellows but no wyverns up there." She nudged her familiar with her cheek.

It emitted a little sound like a half purr, half trill as it pushed its head into her, all three of its little eyes closing gently.

"What kind of shop is this?" Sella asked, trying to sound natural as possible. She glanced around at all the books with careful attention. One could be useful.

Lazil's smile brightened. "Ah, the best part," she said. "This is a bookstore! But unfortunately, no one here reads my home's language… which. Well, most of the books here are. A bit of an oversight, if I'm being honest."

Sella noticed a bit of an accent to her tone now, one she hadn't picked up on before. She wondered if it came and went as some she had known in Orakan. Sella's brow furrowed. "How do you..?"

Lazil waved a hand at her. "Oh, I'm also an elemental witch, but apparently that's frowned upon down south," she said with a laugh as though the idea was absolutely ridiculous. "Good thing this town is one of the more accepting ones. I help the village with their water collection and I can find it underground in the dry months. Honestly, what they did before me is anyone's guess. I suppose everyone just went thirsty."

"Indeed," Poem said dryly. "There's an abundance of witches here for such a small town."

Lazil's happy expression never wavered. She scratched under her familiar's chin. "I help Verol with water, she helps with the plants, the kitchen witches will help turn those plants into remedies and potions. It seems like we have the exact right number of witches."

"We're actually more than that," Sella said. "Back in Orakan we are also a detective agency. I'm sorry, it's actually why we're here today." She looked around at all the books one more time before turning back to Poem. "We wanted to offer up our help."

Poem cocked his head. "Perhaps," he said simply. "The military is quite keen on getting this assassination solved quickly."

"assassination?" Sella pulled back. The word was stronger than she expected and it hit her in the gut hard.

"A prominent member of the military is murdered?" Poem said, his demeanor calm, though it sounded as though he was scolding her. "Yes, Sella, I'd call that an assassination." He paused, studying her carefully. "You could be helpful, though. Since we're both new, we have no ties here. We can be objective. A few wyvern riders should be coming in later today, lightning allowing. Why don't you come and tell us some of your theories and observations." It was worded as a question, but sounded like a command.

Sella did her best to smile when, really, she wanted to grab Beejee and run. She was already tired of his attitude. "We can do that," she said as indifferently as she could.

Poem smiled. "Meet us at the tavern tonight."

She nodded back.

At least Lohrna would love this recent development.

Lazil rested her chin in her hand. She raised a brow at Sella and flashed her a sly half smile. "Look at you, witch of many talents," she said with a wink.

FOURTEEN

The Other Wyvern Rider

"Why do you think he goes by 'Poem'?" Lohrna asked. "That doesn't sound like a name from around here. Oh! Do you think it's a poem unto itself?" The flickering firelight of the little flames overhead lit her face in delicate shadow as the afternoon storm outside pelted the shop with hard rain.

Beejee barred his teeth. "What does it matter? Or even mean? The point is, we've got an abundance of witches in this town and a detective who is clearly just humoring us until he inevitably points the finger in our direction." He looked up at a passing ball of fire. "Sella! Make yourself look less obvious!"

Sella's glance flicked up. She cringed.

Lohrna leaned her head back over the chair. "Oh, Beejee, no one is going to brave the rain, right Cali?"

Cali angled her body so she could look Lohrna in the eyes, though Lohrna couldn't see her. "Probably not," she said. "Things shut down around this time anyway."

"Don't you take her side," Beejee hissed.

Lohrna's smile widened. She sat back up straight and clapped her hands together. "Let's go into tonight with a good mindset," she said just as a rumble of thunder cracked low from outside. Her eyes slowly moved back to the door. "Alright, so that was ominous, but I'm not letting it get to me. We need to go in there and make a good impression and meet these new riders. Who knows, maybe they can give us more details about Baz? Plus," she turned to look in Cali's general direction. "You can float around and pick up any gossip that Sella and I might miss."

Another crack of thunder sounded outside and the rain hit the shop even harder.

"I'm staying here," Beejee said. "I'm not about to step in a bunch of mud just for this. And I could use some respite from the incessant chatter. You people never shut up."

THE STORM HAD CALMED and the sky above was painted in brilliant gold and pink and pastel orange. Sella stared up in awe, trying to make out every colorful nuance, to commit to memory the immense feeling of the sky full of pigment as a chill raced up her arms despite the heat surrounding her.

But Lohrna was holding the door to the tavern open wide for her and Sella was compelled to hustle along inside the tavern.

At her side, Cali smiled. "It's beautiful, isn't it?"

"I wish I could paint it," Sella whispered back.

Cali pushed her arm lightly. "Give it a go," she said. "Who knows, maybe this whole time you're a secret artist."

"Yeah, maybe someday." Sella's eyes traced the wall of the tavern, looking at the few faces to see if she recognized anyone.

Lohrna was already bounding up to the bar, her fingers held up for two drinks.

"I don't think I could capture it if I wanted to," she said honestly. "Maybe Lohr."

Cali shrugged. "You don't give yourself enough space for hobbies," she said.

Sella's chest expanded. "No, that's true." Her gaze caught Poem, sitting at a table with three uniformed humans. She squinted into the dark. Motetzelial and Tateliali, she noted, were seated together, their faces mostly in shadow.

They were all listening to a woman in the same military attire. She had a bright smile, noticeable freckles across her nose as it scrunched a little at whatever joke or story she had just told. The woman ran fingers through her auburn hair, cut close on one side, and cascading down her shoulder on the other.

Sella's heartbeat quickened, a rush of cold ran from her scalp to her toes. The woman looked so familiar. So much like…"Cali…" Sella breathed, reaching for the ghost's hand.

Cali followed Sella's stare to the table, and her smile disappeared in a flash. "Amirisyali… my sister."

"What'd I miss?" Lohrna said, appearing as if by magic at Sella's side. She held a drink to Sella. "Why are we just standing here?"

Sella couldn't pull her eyes away, her arms hung limply as if she had turned to stone.

Beside them, a chair tipped over.

Lohrna jumped, clutching the wooden cups close to her body. "What the— Cal?"

Poem straightened in his seat, though from the sound of the chair flipping, or just noticing them staring, Sella didn't have the space in her mind to question. He was waving them over, looking surprisingly welcoming.

Lohrna held out her second cup again and this time, Sella sucked in a deep breath and took it quickly. Her feet moved her forward despite everything screaming at her to stop and to run the other direction, to hide away with Cali and her friend and Beejee. To leave this desert and never, ever return.

"That's Cali's sister," Sella breathed so low she wasn't sure she had said it aloud at all.

Lohrna's gasp, however, made it clear that she had. Still, she followed Sella quietly, her mouth closed tight, her eyes wide.

"Good evening, Sella," Poem said with a quick grin flashing across his face. "Is this the other kitchen witch?"

In her pocket, Sella's fingers twitched, she looked to Lohrna and took the opportunity to survey the tavern for any signs of Cali. She was nowhere to be found. But that didn't mean she wasn't there. "This is Lohrna," Sella said, though her voice cracked at the end. She coughed lightly. "Excuse me," she mumbled.

Lohrna dashed in to save her. She held Sella's shoulder with a strong hand. "I'm Lohrna," she said. "I'm not a witch, sadly. But I help out in the shop. I have the design eye."

Amirisyali cocked her head, a bit of hair fell into her face. She pushed out an extra chair with her booted foot. "Have a seat," she ordered.

Sella moved her free hand to hold the back of the chair, her grip tight. She wasn't sure if she would fall over if she let go but she didn't want to test it.

Lohrna dragged another chair close by to the table. The rough sound of the wood scraping against the floor brought Sella's mind back to the present.

She let out a small breath, then sank into her seat beside Lohrna.

"You already know Motetzelial and Tateliali," Poem said after taking a small sip of his drink. "And this is Amirisyali. She's here to help oversee the operation here."

Amirisyali thrust a hand to Sella. "Amirisyali. Acting commander of this squadron," she said.

Lohrna reached across Sella's body to grab Amirisyali's hand. She gave it far too many shakes. "Now is probably a good time to tell you that it's going to take a while to pronounce your names correctly," she said with a laugh. "We'll do our best, though."

The two other soldiers smiled, though Tateliali held a hand over his chest in feign offense.

Poem nodded. "I thought as much," he said. "I

haven't had many dealings with folks across the sea, but it does seem to be a trend."

Tateliali leaned forward. "You can call me Tate. All my friends do."

Motetzelial's jaw clenched.

Sella pulled her eyes away, trying to do her best not to look like she was studying him. She was sure just as she was sitting here feeling like she was slowly sinking into the cold ocean, he, too, was feeling his options narrow as time went on. He may not be guilty, he had to know that from the outside, it certainly looked like he was. Or, at least he was the best suspect.

"Motet," he said at last.

Amirisyali's eyes narrowed. She sat taller, one leg bent up to rest on the seat. It was a surprisingly casual gesture. Sella wasn't sure what to make of it. "Amiri," she said with a smirk. "Can you remember that?"

Lohrna nodded. She swallowed a large gulp, her cup clanking against the table a little too loudly. "Oh yes, that's wonderful, thank you. Sorry, all these new faces and names. It's a lot. This is the first time I've left my small town back home."

The corner of Poem's mouth twitched. "Is that so?"

Lohrna pulled her cup close to her. "Oh, we're still really capable detectives." She turned back to Amiri. "Sorry for your loss, by the way."

Amiri blinked slowly. "Don't worry about it."

Lohrna retracted a little. "Well, Sella's been all over Orakan, right, Sella? We're not naive to the ways of things."

Sella's shoulders lifted. Lohrna had pulled her back from the deep, but she still felt cold. Her eyes still darted about, waiting for Cali. "Yes," she said. "I'm a certified kitchen witch. It's a strict process there. It required me to travel, as did my previous employer."

That, and running away from problems and out of money, she could almost hear Beejee hiss at her. She looked to the door to see him sitting in the shadow of a tall man. She smiled, relief flooding into her body. Her chest finally opened fully as she took a true breath in. Cali must have gotten him.

She was safe.

They were safe.

Amiri tapped the table with her knuckle. "That's good to hear," she said. "We wouldn't want anyone in town falling ill to a bad potion."

THE SHEET over Cali's head rippled, the glasses perched over her face nearly falling off with the motion. Sella had found them while rummaging through the drawers in a frenzy, trying to find anything to make Cali feel more comfortable and at home.

Sella bit the inside of her cheek. She hated that she couldn't see Cali's small expressions, little clues about her inner workings. But the ghost had requested the sheet. And Sella suspected, in part, to hide her face.

The group sat in Sella's bed. Sella, with Beejee snuggled in her lap, nestled into the corner while Lohrna stretched out long, her arm draped over her eyes and hair splayed around her head like a pillow.

"What are the odds?" Lohrna groaned. "Cali, how are you holding up?"

Cali shifted again and Sella noticed that where she sat, there was the smallest indent in the comforter. "I don't know what I feel," she said.

Sella held the parchment firm, writing quickly as Cali spoke.

"When I went across the sea," Cali went on, "I was fine with never seeing any of them again." She paused, looking down at her hands under the sheet. "Stars," Cali swore under her breath. "When I left to study numbers and bookkeeping… When I decided I didn't want to go to the military academy, I was fine never seeing them again. If I'm being honest."

A pain in Sella's heart echoed out to her limbs. She didn't write the last part. She wasn't sure she could. She flashed the paper to Lohrna who looked it over with one eye still shut tight.

"Ah, that makes sense," Lohrna said. "You're the youngest, right?"

Cali nodded. "Amirisyali is the first," she said. "I'm the seventh. We didn't really know each other much when I was little. Amirisyali was this mythical figure who showed up sometimes, riding a rare fire-breathing wyvern, and dispensing strange candies from places she had just come back from." She laughed, but it sounded hollow. "That was always the best part about her coming home. Is that awful?"

Sella did her best to write it all, though her handwriting was noticeably worse as she went on.

"I wonder if she missed me at all," Cali breathed. "I don't think I missed her, if I'm being honest."

Sella set the paper down. With one hand, she held Beejee, with the other, she reached beneath the sheet and Cali's fingers laced with hers.

"It's strange," Cali said at last. "To see her again. She doesn't even know I'm dead."

Lohrna finally opened both eyes. She sighed and moved her head toward Sella and Cali. "It kind of feels like it was meant to be, though," she whispered. "As painful as that is."

Cali nodded. Her thumb, cold, and not quite solid, ran across Sella's palm. "It does feel like it was star-fated," she said at last. The sheet turned to Sella. "Even if it was, I wish it hadn't happened."

Sella nodded. She told Lohrna who hummed gently in return, blowing a curl from her face.

"I think you're allowed to feel about it however you feel about it, Cali," Lohrna said slowly. "Should we tell her you're here?"

Cali shook her head. "No," she said. "Not yet."

"When you're ready," Beejee said. "Or not, if you never are."

"Thank you," Cali whispered.

THE REST of the night was sleepless, at least for Sella. She replayed the night over and over again, trying to find something hidden. In something Amiri said, in something Poem said, in the look that Motet would occasionally cast to Tate. She tried to remember the exact words that Cali chose when she spoke about her feelings seeing her sister again after death.

But the ghost had requested that Sella burn the pages with her words on them before they went to sleep and so she had nothing but her own memory, however faulty, to go on.

Cali had disappeared long before Sella flicked her wrist and extinguished the lights overhead. And she was left wondering what tomorrow would bring. A surprise, for sure. But if the fin in the water was a dolphin or a shark, she wasn't sure.

The Useless Bookstore

THE MOMENT SELLA unlocked the shop door, it opened.

She jumped back, grabbing the edge of it before it hit her. "We're open!" Sella cried. "But no scones today."

Poem, his head appearing around the door, smiled. "Oh, no scones needed," he said as he pushed his way into the shop. "But now that I know you're certified, I would like a cup of coffee please. And what is the special today? The sign says to inquire, so inquire I will."

Sella shut the door behind him. She hurried past him and to the counter, trying not to show the headache that had been building behind her eyes.

"Focus blend," she lied. She hadn't thought of a special at all. But it seemed like something he would like, and would put the town at ease if any of them were worried about the recent murder.

For the most part, everyone seemed content that Baz had been the target, or an unfortunate causality of bad luck in the forge, and that they weren't next. She wasn't so sure, in fact she had hoped that they wouldn't have many customers that day.

Poem placed a few gold coins on the counter. Sella took them quickly and began to prepare his drink. "Any updates?" she asked, though her attention was on the mug in front of her. She stirred the focus blend with one hand, and held it tight with the other, trying her best to infuse all the calm and rationality she could.

Poem sat on one of the stools. "Well, death by fire," he said. "Two wyvern riders in town, one who is known to question orders. I'd say the case is fairly clear."

Sella slid the mug to him. She poured her own cup.

"Just need the evidence to be ethical for the arrest," he said. He took a sip of coffee and a small grin flickered across his face. "Perhaps you can get a confession out of one of them. You seem… disarming."

Sella scratched the back of her neck. That was one word she'd never think to use for herself. Her whole life, she'd be the object of fear and distrust. The little witch with fire. So out of control, she had burned her own mother.

She pushed the thoughts aside. "For what it's worth," she said, trying to clear the memories from the front of her mind, "Lohrna and I spoke with them before. Motet was very upfront about being there, or at least in the vicinity at the time, and about his argument with Baz. I don't think he'd volunteer that information if he was guilty."

"The truth always comes to light, Sella," Poem said.

"Some people think it's best to control what little they have left in the dark."

Sella's gaze shifted to her own drink. She stared into the black liquid, watching the steam rise up, filling her lungs with warm cinnamon and nutmeg. "Their wyverns don't breathe fire," she said.

Poem tilted his mug to her. "And there's the catch, isn't it? But they are hesitant to talk to me. They know who employs me and how dire their situation is about to become. If you think they're innocent, I'm going to say it's on you to prove it."

Sella sighed. She wasn't sure they were innocent at all. But Lohrna seemed to think so, and she couldn't let two people go down for something they didn't do. Even if Baz was a tyrant. Even if she wasn't sure they were any different. "Alright," she said at last. "We'll do our best to get to the truth of this."

Poem finished the last of his coffee with a long drink. "This was good," he said, rising from his seat with a small groan. He gave her one nod. "Out into the light."

LOHRNA AND BEEJEE, begrudgingly and enthusiastically, elected to stay in the shop. There was still decorating to be done, as Lohnra had promised. And as Beejee pointed out, a lot of business if they put up a sign that they were selling a daily special of luck.

Sella knew they were right. They did have a duty to Sediri, however much that annoyed her, and to the town itself. It wasn't exactly fair to close up when people needed them most.

Still, she wished they were here with her. Sella never could hide her expressions well and fumbled over her words when she was nervous. That, or she simply said the wrong thing entirely. She was surprised they trusted her to go get information on her own.

"You're nervous?"

Sella did her best to smile. "A little," she said quietly as they turned the corner leading out toward the barn at the edge of the town. "No where near what you must be feeling."

Cali shrugged. "I've had time to process it."

Sella raised a brow. "Cali, I know you're good at putting things in your mind aside but… I don't think this is something you can just 'process' overnight."

Cali skipped along for a few steps, quickly moving ahead of Sella. "Am I curious about how she's been and if she wonders about me? Or how everyone else is doing? Sure… But if I was alive and here, and saw her at that table..? I can't say I wouldn't have dashed away in that scenario, too."

"That's fair," Sella sighed out. "But it's more complicated now."

"I recognize that." Cali's tone was harsh.

Sella flinched, but kept pace with her. "Thank you for coming," she said, honestly.

Cali stopped.

The air was still, and all was quiet.

Sella watched as Cali's hands twitched to fists. She

shook them out just as quickly and looked up at the sky with a sigh. "Can you make me something to feel like home tonight?" she asked.

Sella crossed the space between them, the hem of her skirt fluttered quickly around her ankles as she took long steps. She held Cali's hands in hers delicately, as though they'd break. "Like home?"

Cali's eyes shifted across the sky until, finally, they landed on Sella. Her expression softened. "I miss home," she whispered and leaned into Sella's collarbone. "*This* isn't home."

"I'll make you something that feels like home," Sella promised. *And I will find you something that makes you feel like… you.* She kept the last part quiet for now. It was a promise, but one she knew would hurt both of them until it was fulfilled.

Cali pulled away, her hands slipped from Sella's and she pushed at her face with her knuckles. "Alright," she said. "Let's go find some answers." She set out into the open field again as though nothing had happened.

"You're sure?" Sella asked.

Cali waved a hand to her. "Come on, don't make me drag you."

Sella let out a little laugh, and sped up to catch her.

THE SOLDIERS WERE easy to find. At least, their wyverns were. A commotion behind the barn broke the silence. A growl, a thud, and a few angry cries erupted into the air.

Sella and Cali hurried to the other side to see the four wyverns, flapping their wings and snapping their jaws in the air, though all their feet remained grounded.

Sella shielded her eyes from the gusts of wind that blew dust about them with each furious flap of their wings.

Amiri shouted a command and the beating of wings ceased instantly. "There. I told you I could do it," she bragged to Tate and Motet as she put one hand on her hip and tossed her auburn hair with a sweep of her head.

Tate clapped, seemingly with sincerity, though not with enthusiasm, while Motet simply crossed his arms and closed his eyes with a head shake.

"May I inquire?" Sella asked loudly.

Amiri turned to her with a hard stare. "Ah, the kitchen witch," she said.

"Sella," Cali corrected.

"I'm sorry for intruding." Sella moved slowly closer with her hands held up.

"You have nothing to apologize for," Cali added.

Sella shot her a quick look, hoping she didn't look like she had gone mad. "I wanted to see if we could talk a bit more about the wyverns," she lied. "It's just, we're leaving town soon and we don't have anything like this in Orakan. Lohrna's fascinated."

Amiri narrowed her eyes. Her other hand brushed her hair back. "Well, where is she then?"

Tate laughed. "Don't be like that, Amirisyali," he said. "The folks are excited about something new."

Amiri's mouth twerked up, but it wasn't a smile. That

much was clear. "Well, I just bet these two fools a glass of crushed ice that I could calm Lucanairi after a lunch frenzy. It took one word."

Sella took a few steps closer, into the shadow of the large barn. It was instantly cooler here in the shade and relief tickled the back of her neck. "What word?"

Amiri widened her stance. "Ancient tongue of our people," she said, clear that she was inviting no more questions.

Sella nodded, trying to look impressed. She supposed she was, underneath it all. But mostly, she was confused at how different Amiri and Cali were, despite their similar outward appearances. It was striking and she felt off balance. She figured that she may as well keep trying her luck. "Can I buy all of you a round of ice? I would love to talk more, but the heat is taking it out of me. I'm not used to this much sun."

"Tell her you can eat them in the bookstore," Cali whispered.

Sella's eyes flashed to Cali, then to the ground.

"She used to love books." Cali shrugged back.

"We can eat them in the bookstore," Sella said with a smile. "If you like ancient languages, this place doesn't have many books in our own. You might find a hidden gem."

Amiri's shoulders softened. Just a little. Just enough. She took a few steps toward Sella, then waved at the two soldiers to follow. "Why didn't you tell me there was a bookstore?" she barked at them.

Motet walked backwards, keeping his eyes on the

wyverns who had busied themselves with digging at the dirt. "It's run by a witch who didn't consider that none of the books she stocks are in a language anyone here can read," he said. "It didn't seem relevant."

Amiri scoffed. "We'll see."

The group, with the two uniformed men trailing behind, made their way into the market quickly. Sella found the booth with crushed ice and ordered five.

"Four," Cali said as she leaned over the wood to get a better look at the woman scooping large spoonfuls of ice into cups.

"Four, sorry," Sella said quickly.

"I do miss this though," Cali said with a heavy sigh. "And there's really no smell most of the time. Such a shame."

"I'm sorry," Sella said, her tone so somber that the woman behind the counter looked up from her work with a deep worry line forming between her brows.

"Four, not five," the woman said with a smile slowly building across her face as she went back to her work. "It's not forgetting to trap the spring."

"It means 'it's not a big issue', or, like, 'not a big worry'," Cali translated.

Sella mouthed a 'thank you', then a louder one to the woman as she handed out the crushed ice.

Amiri grabbed hers quickly. She scooped several spoonfuls into her mouth before she looked around them. "Where's this bookstore?"

Tate shoved his mouthful to one side and spoke with a

half closed mouth, "This way." He pointed out of the market and toward the storm clouds forming.

"Will we be rained in?" Sella asked. Her own cup was melting slowly in her hands.

Amiri squinted into the sky. "No," she said. "It won't rain today."

"Too high up," Tate explained. "When they look like that, all flat and not puffy, it means they won't make it this far."

Motet shielded his eyes and stared up. His own crushed ice dripped from the side. "Unlikely," he said. "But I wouldn't be so sure."

Sella did her best to simply nod but she had to admit, there was something strange about Motet. He had a way of quietly disagreeing with everyone.

She simply took a bite of her ice, and sighed with relief at the sudden coolness flooding her mouth and throat. She savored the sweet, subtle flavor of the chopped fruit on top. It was like nothing she had experienced before, almost floral. She swallowed several more bites quickly, grateful for the instantly soothing effect it had on her in the hot sun. The woman may not have been a kitchen witch, but this felt like a unique kind of magic.

They finished their treats quickly, occasionally looking up at the clouds again and commenting on if they were approaching or not and if it would actually rain.

Sella hurried to give the cups back, with Cali right at her side. "We should ask about the argument," she said. "But, you know, make it sound natural."

"Easy," Sella said sarcastically.

Cali rolled her eyes but nudged Sella's arm playfully. "Maybe sound worried?"

Sella nodded. That she could do.

As the group left the market, Sella leaned closer to Tate and Motet. "Do you think the killer is still in town? There's so rarely anything like this where I'm from. Are we in danger?"

Motet's stare ahead hardened. "I don't think we're in danger," he said. "It was probably a fire in the forge. Got out of control."

Tate raised a finger. "Or a witch," he said. "Baz sure did make a lot of witches angry."

Sella pretended to consider it. She glanced at Amiri who was watching them closely from her peripherals as they continued walking. Sella went on, "But there's only the hedge witch, a water witch, and me here."

"A kitchen witch?" Amiri clarified.

Sella let out a breath. "Certified," both she and Cali added. Sella stopped in front of the bright blue door of the narrow little shop. "We're here."

"That's it for me for now," Cali said. She shimmered from Sella's sight. "I'll go snoop around the market."

Sella gave one small nod.

"Don't let my sister bully you," Cali's voice warned. "She can be intense but... I think she's kind underneath."

Sella tapped the fake wand in her pocket and led the way into the shop.

. . .

LAZIL GREETED them all as warmly as she had the last time Sella had been in the shop. It didn't surprise her, necessarily, but most of the interactions Sella had observed with the military here had been cold.

As Sella pretended to browse books, she did her best to listen in on their conversation and only kicked herself a little at not coming here sooner.

"Well, I have a shop full of books no one can read," Lazil explained as her familiar crept down her arm and onto the counter, all of its little legs in unison. "But I make a modest living all the same with my elemental magic. I'm here for adventure and because of foolishness. We never did get an answer on why *you* are here."

The way she said it sounded so natural and conversational. Sella tried to dissect what it was about Lazil that had the effect when almost everything Sella said sounded prying or uncomfortable.

Perhaps it was her easy smile. Sella had a very forced expression most of the time.

Tate was leaning on the counter, holding a single finger out for the familiar to sniff. "Routine patrol," he said. "Orders come from up top. We follow them."

Lazil laughed and motioned to Amiri who was standing in the corner, an open book in hand. "And aren't you the 'up top'?"

Amiri closed the book. "I'll take this one," she said, ignoring the question entirely.

"It's written in the language of the north," Lazil warned.

Amiri smirked, that same look she gave almost everyone. As if she liked being set up to show off. She crossed the store with a few confident steps. "Letetsho ohin," she said confidently, her tone changed with the new language on her lips.

From the corner of Sella's eye, she watched as Lazil flinched, but recovered with a bright customer service smile. "Ah, it's been a while since I've heard my old tongue." She took the book and wrapped it in a silk cloth with tenderness in her hands. "Ohin neshin."

SIXTEEN

Home is Where the Tea Towel Is

IT WAS dark by the time Sella made it back to the room above the potions shop. She was tired, but the work had only just begun. She fumbled to open the door into their temporary home, a large basket overflowing with herbs and spices and anything else she could find at the market, balanced precariously on her hip.

She pushed the door open, far harder than she intended to, and the sound of it smacking the wall, made the whole room jump.

"Sorry," she said as she shut the door with her foot. "Everyone doing alright up here?"

Cali, with her sheet over her head, rose from the table. The sheet cascaded to the floor and she appeared at Sella's side.

"Beejee's been a great translator," Lohrna said. "Plus, business was surprisingly good. You'll have to hire me when we get back to Marra! I'm excellent at upselling."

Beejee sat up from his loafed position on the table.

"Business *was* good. Until you spent it all!" He jumped from the table to the counter where Sella was busy laying out her purchases. "What in all the oceans is all this?"

Sella shooed him away with a wave of her hand but he dodged her and continued sniffing at the various plants. When she got to the bottom of the basket, pulling free a new red and yellow towel with two embroidered wyverns in flight, he yowled.

"Sella! You've never been good with money but this is excessive!" He turned to Cali. "Tell her! Tell her to return it all!"

Cali stared at it all, a smile slowly reaching the corners of her eyes. "Home," she whispered.

"Oh, Beejee," Lohrna called from her seat. She leaned forward and rested her head in her hands. "Come on, let her live a little. We've traveled so far. She deserves to spend a little on herself."

"Besides," Sella said, sorting her purchases, "I traded for a lot of it. Some people will be coming tomorrow for free scones infused with our lavender honey. The batch we brought over."

Beejee's eyes narrowed. But he simply thrust his head to the side, clearly still upset, but out of argument.

Outside, a crack of thunder shook the shutters just as rain began to fall heavy against the windows. It almost sounded like music to Sella. Like a strong beat of a drum.

So Motet had been right.

She wondered if Amiri was growling at herself for publicly saying it wasn't going to rain. It seemed like something she'd be hung up on, though trivial to Sella.

She wasn't sure where Amiri learned the need to constantly prove herself, or why she often did it at the expense of others, but she knew that the 'hit first before anyone could question' attitude had to have come from somewhere.

A burst of lighting shook her thoughts.

"Go sit," Sella told Cali and Beejee. "I'll fill you in on what I learned while I make us dinner and get the scones ready for tomorrow."

THE ROOM WAS CRADLED in the warmth of the little fires and the smell of savory roasted nuts and crisp fruits slowly melting and caramelizing in the clay oven in the wall. Sella had given her news, though there wasn't much to really give, and was busy brewing up the second pot of tea. This time, infused with joy and security.

Lohrna was still busy eating at the table. She said with a mouthful, "Well, everyone here's incredibly nice. For the most part. Someone asked to touch my horns, though. That was odd."

"I still can't believe you let them," Beejee said.

Lohrna shrugged, chewing slowly.

"Did you find out anything that might help out with the case?" Sella asked.

Beejee spoke before Lohrna could mumble through her chewing. "Poem is a shifter," he said. "Doesn't take suppressants. Doesn't believe in them, he says."

Sella heated the metal pot in her hands. "That doesn't exactly surprise me," she said. "He seems to have a natural distrust of witches." Her expression soured. "So do the military, though."

Cali shrugged beneath the sheet. "Power against power," she said simply. "They usually get along just fine. But just like anything, there's prejudice sometimes."

Sella brought the tea over and poured three mugs. "They don't recruit witches?"

"Seems like the obvious thing to do," Beejee said. "Consolidate the power."

Cali shook her head. "There's an old story about an elemental witch who rode a wyvern. She could direct the fire, wield it on her own. I don't remember how it went, exactly... but it didn't end well." She paused, leaning down to smell the silver steam rising from the new yellow mug Sella had bought.

Lohrna patiently sipped from her own pink cup. She tapped it with a nail, making the sound like the rain back home, light and calm and rhythmic while the storm outside raged on. "Just like home," she murmured with a small smile as the tea took effect.

Cali went on at last, sitting up straighter. "I'm not even sure if the story is true, or if it's propaganda, or a legend told to children. But there are very few witches serving now, if any."

"They don't trust us and we don't trust them," Beejee said.

Lohrna raised a brow. "What's this now?"

Sella slumped in her seat. She was glad that the two of them were feeling safe and warm and home, but she couldn't shake the feeling of home for her being an absolute mess. "There's an old tale about an elemental witch controlling fire and using it for something awful with her wyvern," she grumbled, eyes closing slowly. "And so there's not many witch and military overlap."

Lohrna hummed as she considered it. "Any shifters?"

Cali shrugged. "Not sure," she said. "Most here take the suppressant. So while they're more common, they're not as known by most of us."

Sella shook her head.

Lohrna sighed. "There goes my career aspirations," she said dryly.

Cali laughed.

Sella snorted.

And even Beejee's whiskers twitched.

SEVENTEEN

Sella Just Got Here

THE MORNING WAS SO clear and dry that if Sella had not heard the thunder and the hammering rain all night, she would have never believed it happened at all.

Poem was in the shop, once again squeezing his way through at the exact moment they opened. Sella had half the thought to tell him to stop being so weird standing outside the building, but she kept her mouth shut and instead got to work brewing a pot of coffee and setting out the honey scones that filled the shop with the sweet scent of crystallized sugar and calming lavender.

Poem placed one hand in the pocket of his baggy pants and casually crossed the shop, looking at each item along the wall and still unopened crates, as if he had never been in before.

Sella did her best to stand up straight and smile brightly as she stirred in the calming blend to his drink. "Good morning, Poem," she said, her voice a bit higher than usual.

"Any information for me?" he asked as he took a seat at the bar.

Straight to business, then.

Sella shook her head. "Not really, unfortunately. They were here on a routine mission. And they seem to think it's a witch that did it."

Poem raised a graying brow.

Sella slid a cup of steaming coffee toward him slowly. She added, "I explained that there's just the three of us here, though. Verol is a hedge witch, she works with plants and growing things. Lazil works with water. And I'm a certified kitchen witch. So unless someone is hiding, it seems unlikely."

Poem took the mug and nodded, mostly to himself, it seemed. He took a small sip then looked Sella in the eyes. "Yes, they were keen to share that opinion with me as well," he said. "Though the most logical cause would have to be wyvern fire, don't you suppose?"

Sella's mouth pulled to one side. She pretended to be distracted by setting the scones out just right, tweaking them this way and that so the drizzle of hardened honey caught the light. "I suppose so," she said. "Why do they think it's witches... do you think?" Her gaze lifted a little.

Poem leaned back. He took another long sip as Sella reached below the counter for the jar of dried lavender. "Amirisyali has been looking to take over this region for some time, did you know?"

Surprise flashed across her face before she could control it. "No, she didn't open up to me much."

Poem's eyes watched her carefully. "Her wyvern breathes fire," he said.

A cold climbed up her back, prickled at her skin like spider legs. She scratched her back as light-heartedly as she could, hopeful that it didn't look like she was trying to soothe herself from the shocking information. "Are you sure?" Her voice was steady, her eyes fixed on the scones.

"Positive," Poem said.

THE FEELING of dread had yet to leave Sella's bones as the day wore on. Customers, many of whom were from the market the night before and here for their traded scones, came and went. Some stayed and talked at length, asking questions about her home, her horns around her ears, if she thought the murder was politically motivated.

To the last, she simply shrugged and said bluntly, "I just got here."

When Rae and Echori entered, Sella felt the hint of relief take hold of her heart. At least she was familiar with these faces.

The two sat at the counter and ordered whatever Sella recommended. To which, she merely added an extra dose of compassion to their mugs and called it good.

The two humans drank quietly, eyeing the scones occasionally.

"Lavender honey from my home," Sella said with a kind smile. She pulled a plate from below the counter and offered one to them. "They're a special recipe."

Echori picked off a corner of the scone, inspecting it

in the light carefully. "It looks great," he said. He sniffed. "Smells even better."

Sella let out a little laugh. "I promise it tastes good, too," she said. She gestured for him to try it. "I'm certified, nothing scary in there. And no charge. Free sample."

Echori smiled and popped the bite into his mouth. He nodded at Rae and moved the scone closer to her.

She picked off another corner and chewed slowly. "It's good," she said as she reached for another sip of her coffee. "Will you be giving this recipe to the other kitchen witch when she returns?"

Sella nodded. "I don't see why not," she said with a little shrug. "I couldn't serve these then leave you all without."

The humans smiled and ate the rest of their scone in a quiet contentment.

Sella moved along the counter to the last few crates that lingered on the shop floor. She stood, staring at them with her hands on her hips. She wasn't really sure where to begin with any of it. But she wanted to be helpful. Lohrna had been working hard to get things set up here, and to cover for her with the investigation. It was only right that she tried to return the favor.

"Do you have any leads?" Rae finally asked, her voice strong from the other side of the shop.

Sella turned to her quickly. She shook her head. "Not yet."

"Well, work faster."

Sella flinched.

Beejee sprung up from the shadows to her side.

"Watch yourself! You are in the presence of a great witch!"

Rae's eyes only flashed at him a moment, then they set on Sella again. "I'm not trying to be unkind," she said.

Beejee hissed.

Echori jumped in, his hands raised in surrender. "We're only worried. There's talk that the detective is honing in on the witches here."

A sting hit Sella like a slap. She curled her fingers on the counter. "I… I don't think he is," she said. Had he lied? Or did something new happen between their morning conversation and now? She tried to replay their conversation, his expressions, but her heart was beating too rapidly to focus properly.

Echori held his mug tightly. "That's the rumor. And we care about Verol."

"And Lazil," Rae added, her words rushed. "She has saved this town from drought many times since her arrival."

Sella wasn't sure what had happened, but she knew she needed to get ahead of it. "Thank you for the information," she said. "Where did you hear these rumors?"

EIGHTEEN

The Night Market

THE NIGHT AIR was warm and fragrant as the steam from booths in the market carried the scent of rich spices, and candied fruits. Intricate textiles hung from the wooden racks all along the left side of the aisle. And as a breeze blew down the narrow alley of tables and goods, the musical sound of glass beads and metals swaying and clinking together gently filled the night. They mixed with the din of the people selling, buying, and socializing.

This was the busiest Sella had seen the market and it seemed that extra rows of tables had been brought out to turn the once wide rows into a narrow labyrinth. She suspected she would feel overwhelmed, if not for the novelty of it all that kept her going.

Her eyes bounced from brightly colored blanket, to hanging necklaces, to brilliant fruits, and over to a man laughing loudly behind the booth, shaking something in his pan that hissed and a sudden burst of fire ignited in the cast iron.

The group around the booth all cheered and the fire extinguished quickly.

Sella's gaze darkened.

At her side, Cali's voice whispered, "It's a tradition. They use a kind of oil to make a quick burst of fire and ignite the meat. It's a quick way to cook it."

"Well that's fun and mildly suspicious!" Lohrna said in Sella's other ear. "Should we go try some? It smells amazing."

Sella had to admit, it really did.

At her feet, Beejee looked up. "It wouldn't hurt to go try some and ask how the fire works," he said.

Sella glanced down at him with a half smile. "I thought we were supposed to be saving money?"

Lohrna grabbed Sella's hand and led her through the small crowd. "Never question Beejee," she said with a laugh. "Come on!"

The man stationed at the booth looked up at them as she entered the periphery of the group. He smiled, his sweat-beaded face cracking with deep wrinkles. It looked to Sella like he had spent his many years happy, and working. He ran the back of his forearm across his brow and served up the sizzling meat to the small group of humans with a large wooden spatula.

They said their thanks, some glancing a little too long at Sella and Lohrna, before they moved on to their next destination.

"Well, I never thought I'd see another Wylde in my time," he said with a deep belly laugh. He leaned down to pull more meat and spices from beside the small firepit he had built into the clay ground.

Lohrna thrust her hand forward but the man waved her off.

"Oh, no need for that here," he said. He showed his hands, bent fingers and callused palms. "I never did like that pleasantry, but I commend you for learning it." The meat crackled as soon as it hit the pan. "No spice for the cat, am I right?"

Sella smiled, her body suddenly lighter. "Right," she said, though it was lost in the music of the market.

"How is this made?" Lohrna asked, leaning in a little so he could hear her clearly.

The man nodded to her to come closer. He held a dark bottle up for her. "Take just a bit of this," he said. His skilled movement held the heavy pan up and flipped the contents with a single motion. "Add a splash." The pan was up even higher now as he lifted his other arm up and dramatically added just a little to the pan.

Their faces illuminated in bright orange as the pan caught fire for a moment, then extinguished just as quickly, covering them in low shadows again.

Lohrna's mouth hung open as he served them in little wooden bowls. He shuffled around the booth to let Beejee take his straight from his spoon.

Lohrna wasted no time eating hers. Her eyes shut as she chewed quickly. From the side of her mouth she called out, "This is amazing!"

The old man moved back behind his booth and smiled. "An old family recipe," he said.

Sella fished coins from her pocket, but at the sound of the metal, the man waved his hand. "No need. Your payment can be gossip. Tell me, how are things in Orakan?"

Sella smiled, but retrieved the coins anyway. "I'm afraid there is little to tell. The king is the same as the one since you visited, I'm sure."

The man nodded, stretching his back as he held onto the wooden counter between them. "And will be long after I am gone."

Sella's eyes softened. "We're from Marra, a small port town. We don't bother the rest of Orakan, and they leave us be for the most part."

Lohrna swallowed and handed the man the bowl back. "But we did host the Opora last year! And the Golden Ladle was stolen. A mayor died. And we discovered a new society of shifters running around the place preaching weird rules." Her words flooded from her. "I mean, not a lot has happened, but I've gotten the most adventure in the past few years than I ever thought I'd see!"

Both Sella and the man chuckled at her enthusiasm. That is, until Sella noticed Cali behind the counter, leaning down to study the bottle he had used.

She did her best to keep her expression light and pulled her eyes away from the ghost quickly. She raised her hand. "I'm Sella," she said. "This is Lohrna and Beejee."

"Call me Cosas," the man said with a wink.

"What should we try next?" Lohrna asked, her excitement shining brightly.

Cosas pointed down the narrow path. "Last booth on this row," he said. "The water witch is selling water from the high mountains. It's a luxury, even for you, I would wager."

Lazil.

Sella leaned back to see if she could make out the booth but it was too crowded. "All the way at the end?" she asked.

"All the way down," he said. "I suspect she's avoiding the wyvern riders."

"Why's that?" Lohrna asked. It sounded innocent.

Cosas smiled, but his eyes were suddenly tired.

Another group of humans pushed forward. A few exclaimed his full name with happiness and humor in their tone.

The man nodded at them. "It's good to visit old memories," he said quietly before turning his attention to the other group.

"Let's go," Cali said, materializing beside Sella. "That fire enhancer is strong, but I don't think it's strong enough to do what happened to Baz."

Sella used the distraction of the other people to leave three gold coins on the counter and they slipped away.

As they mingled back into the crowd, Lohrna asked, "So, best meat ever, right? But what about the fire?"

Sella shook her head. "Cali doesn't think it's enough to make a fire big enough to do it," she said.

Lohrna's shoulders slumped, her head fell back. "Oh

thank the tides!" She perked back up quickly. "I don't think I could have it in my heart to send an old man who makes such delicious foods away. That'd be a travesty."

"As opposed to the travesty of a man dying?" Beejee said.

Sella rolled her eyes. He was just being a contrarian.

At least Lohrna seemed to notice. "A man who burns down barns for no reason and bullies everyone around him? Or a man who uses his skill to conjure up delicacies and enjoys good gossip? I know who I'm rooting for."

"I'll go see what I can," Cali said. "I'm not really ready for another witch to see me just yet."

"Can I tell her?" Sella asked quietly. "That way you don't need to be there for the shock of it?"

Cali nodded. "If you're up for it. That'd be helpful." She slipped back the way they had come, disappearing into the crowd.

Sella smiled. She was glad to be helpful, even in the smallest way.

The last booth at the end of the row was quiet, though it seemed from Lazil's posture that they may have just missed a rush of people. She looked tired.

"Everything alright?" Sella asked.

Lazil straightened and did her best to grin pleasantly. The familiar on her shoulder, however, seemed less willing to hide its emotions. Its three eyes closed slowly, and it huffed a little.

"We're fine," Lazil said. "It's good to see you, Sella. Lohrna. Beejee." She took turns addressing each with a little nod.

"Good to finally meet you!" Lohrna bounded to the table. "I heard you've been a real help to this town since you got here."

Lazil's smile grew genuine.

It was impossible, it seemed, to deny Lohrna's joy.

Lazil rubbed the back of her shaved head. "Is your ghost still frightened of me?" she asked as she leaned to one side, looking for Cali.

Sella pulled back. "I… No, it's not that–"

"Verol told me," Lazil explained. "I hope that wasn't breaking her confidence. It's just…"

Sella watched her closely. She seemed uncharacteristically nervous. Every other time she had seen the witch, she had appeared effortlessly friendly.

Lazil went on, "Verol wanted to prepare me. Usually we banish spirits from this existence, do we not?"

Lohrna held out a hand to Lazil. "Cali's special. You'll see when you meet her."

Sella nodded. "She's unlike any ghost I've ever seen. And I have seen a few."

Lazil's expression softened. "I have been lucky enough to not meet a single one." She flinched at her own words. "Sorry, I would like to meet *your* ghost, I didn't mean it like that."

Sella took Lazil's hand and gave it a small squeeze. "No, I understand. They're rare." She let go quickly. "She'll be glad to know that she doesn't need to hide anymore."

Lazil's familiar climbed down her arm. He peered over the table top to look at Beejee. It trilled lightly.

Beejee's ears pulled back. "But Baz isn't like Cali. He didn't come back as a ghost," Beejee told the creature.

Lazil's attention shifted. She craned her neck down to look at Beejee. "That's true," she said. "But it's worth a try to look through the texts. There are stories of spells in my culture to raise spirits, temporarily. They're used for loved ones to say their goodbyes when the death is unexpected. We could take a look."

A sudden flood of excitement ignited Sella's limbs. "Wait, there's a spell for ghosts to talk?"

Lazil cocked her head to one side. "I've heard of it. It could definitely help the case, but it's not a guarantee that I have the right book."

Lohrna grabbed Sella's arm. "It's worth a try."

Sella smiled, relief and fear in equal parts.

They had come to the market to hear rumors and theories and left with so much more. They had come to Sunfall to help Sediri and found themselves in yet another mess beyond their control. But Sella had also come here for knowledge. The kind she couldn't find back home. And perhaps, just maybe, she thought, she had stumbled her way into something good.

NINETEEN

A Spell for Speaking

LAZIL STUMBLED through the door to the potions shop, a stack of books riskily balanced from her waist and piled up over her head swayed as if they were all about to topple over. She ducked to one side to see Sella and smiled brightly.

"Good morning!" Her head hid behind the stack again as Sella hurried to help. "Oh, no need," she said, making her way with practiced steps to the small table.

"I'll make you something," Sella said. "Focus blend?"

"That would be helpful." Lazil was already starting to sort through her books, making little piles on the floor. "I'm not saying this will work," she reminded Sella. "I'm just a collector and lover of words. But I have to admit, I don't know what's in half of these books."

"But it's worth a try," Sella said just as a prickle traced up her spine. She turned to see Cali beside her with a wide grin.

Lazil paused her work, one hand still hovered over a

book stack. She turned her head slowly toward them. "Calisyali?"

Cali stepped closer to Sella but she nodded her head. "Just Cali is fine," she said, her voice trembling at the end.

Sella's hand reflexively grabbed Cali's. It was cold but solid.

Lazil uncurled herself from her crouch to stand tall. She smiled, warm and kind. "I'm not going to banish you," she said. "I wouldn't even know the spell for that. I'm just excited to meet you at last. Did Sella tell you why I'm here?"

Cali nodded. "You're looking for a spell to bring Baz back."

"Only temporarily, if the stories are true." Lazil's eyes bounced from Cali to Sella. She closed them slowly, before opening them again with a long sigh. You look familiar," she said at last.

"Amirisyali is my sister," Cali said. She let go of Sella's hand and propped herself on the counter. "You met her?"

Lazil's eyes widened. "I have," she said. She followed Cali's cue and sat at the table, the tension in her body loosening a little. "She could be of some help today, actually. Though I doubt her willingness." She grabbed the first book and began to shift through its pages before glancing back up. "There's no chance you read the language of the north, is there?"

Cali shook her head. "Sadly, no."

"But if you need any math or small details looked at," Sella said as she poured two cups of coffee as the rich aroma of caramel and dark grounds filled the small space, "Cali's your ghost."

Lazil went back to her reading. "Good to know," she said. She sniffed loudly. "I'll take the focus blend, now."

IT HAD BEEN quiet the rest of the early morning.

Lohrna was busy painting little flowers along the walls and shelves. Splashes of paint streaked across her arms and cheeks, but she was careful with the places that mattered.

Each little bright flower and scaling green vine was done with purpose and joy. She leaned in so her nose almost touched the wall to get the details done with precision.

Beejee and Cali chatted occasionally with Lazil, mostly when she needed to bounce an idea off of someone, like: "Do you think that a spell to learn any language would be helpful?" or "What about a spell to bring back a dead houseplant?"

The answers being "No, if it's just speaking" – it was. And "No, but why just *house*plants in particular?" – to which Lazil merely shrugged and went back to reading.

Sella felt that something was off. Lazil every other time had been chipper and charming. Now, she seemed studious and as though she didn't care at all to make much casual conversation.

Her suspicions only amplified when Poem walked through the door.

As she did her best to feign a smile, Lazil looked up at

him from her table with a deep glare before hiding her face back in the book.

Poem didn't seem to notice her at all. He crossed the shop and Sella handed him a mug ready for him. "Focus," she said confidently. "Caramel and honey notes."

Poem set his coins down and took a long sip. Only then did his eyes flash to Lazil. "A bookclub?" he asked.

"Rude," Cali said.

Lohrna looked up from her corner of the shop, her paintbrush still hovering over the latest batch of lavender.

Beejee nodded in agreement but stayed quiet.

"We are looking for a spell," Sella said slowly. She knew better now than to trust him. But, she supposed it would be better to have him in the know about the spell, just in case it worked. She didn't want it to be the witches' word against… nothing at all. She went on, "An ancient spell to bring back the dead for a few moments."

Poem sipped his coffee as if that was exactly what he expected her to say. He nodded. "I'd like to be there when you summon him," he said at last.

Sella and Lazil's eyes met for a moment.

"Of course," Sella said.

Lazil cringed.

"I think it's important we are all hearing the same things," Sella said, for both Poem and Lazil's benefit.

It was quiet for a long moment until the door opened with a loud thud.

Sella was certain that the door would have broken hinges by the time Sediri came back. She made a note to ask Cali if it was custom to just show up everywhere dramatically or if humans really were always in such a hurry that they broke things in the process.

Amiri filled the space in the doorway, seeming much larger than Sella knew she was. She filled the space with a broad stance and looked around the room with green eyes shining until they landed on Lazil.

"Oh, I didn't expect there to be such a crowd," she said, her voice suddenly easy. She strode into the shop, her eyes surveying everyone from Lohrna at the floor, to Beejee. Sella noticed that they lingered on Poem for just a moment too long.

Sella did her best to pretend not to notice. The soldier was watching the detective, keeping him close. But why? She poured a cup of coffee to distract herself from spiraling. "Focus blend?" she offered Amiri.

Amiri sat at one of the barstools, her body angled out to keep everyone in her line of sight and her front to the door. "Anything stronger?"

Sella pulled the mug back and got to work on another fresh brew. She grabbed a bottle labeled 'Don't Strangle People', a compassion and patience blend, and another small jar of 'Who Needs Sleep?'.

She wasn't exactly sure if one would cancel the other out, but if Amiri wanted a stronger brew, this was probably the best bet.

She wrapped her hands around the metal pot and it warmed at her touch. She focused her energy on sending healing and love to Cali's sister. Amiri didn't know what had happened to her youngest sibling, but she could still give back a little love that Cali held for her in a mug.

When she was done, she handed the mug to Amiri with a warm smile.

"Can you read the northern language?" Lazil asked, her eyes peeked out over the top of the book she had opened on the table.

Amiri nodded. She sipped from her mug but the drink was so small, Sella wasn't sure she could taste it at all. "Why do you ask?"

Lazil looked back down. "I just want to be sure the book you purchased will be read. Some people can only speak, they cannot read." Her eyes flicked back up as if waiting to see if the undercut insult landed.

Amiri smiled a half, wolfish grin. She cast her gaze to Poem again. "And you, detective? What do you read?"

Poem let out a small chuckle. "I'm afraid I have no time to read these days," he said.

Amiri tossed her head to one side. "I'm afraid of that as well," she said under her breath.

TWENTY

The Bee is Not Really a Bee

IT WAS GROWING dark in the shop. Lazil had long left, carrying all of her books back out with her and insisting that she didn't need help getting them home. She promised to keep looking, and come back for more coffee in the morning.

Poem had left with Amiri close behind and no one else entered the shop after. Sella had just been considering closely a little early when Beejee's lips curled into a snarl as he rushed to the door of the shop with quick, light feet.

"What is it?" Cali asked, pushing herself off the counter to join him.

Beejee looked up at her. "A grackle," he hissed. "I'd know those wing flaps anywhere."

"Sediri's familiar?" Sella's heart quickened at the thought. She felt like a little kid who had been tasked with something important and had failed to follow through. And, in a way, she had. The signature potion wasn't ready yet. There was even still some painting to be done in the shop. It was a mess. Sella shook the thoughts from her head. "Wait, she's back early… Why is she–"

Beejee leaped backwards as the door burst open with a loud *bang*. The excited flutter of bird wings filled the space and Sediri was already speaking as she stepped inside.

"Sella," she said, tossing a lock of red hair behind her shoulder. With long nailed fingers, she waved her hand up and down Sella's figure. "May I ask why every time we meet someone ends up dead?"

Sella shrugged. "No one died at the certification exam." Still, her gaze went back to the door, she studied the old brass hinges, surprised they had been able to continue to withstand their assaults.

Sediri rolled her eyes exaggeratedly. "Ridiculous," she muttered as she smoothed her dress. "I had to cut my vacation short to come back here and try to clean this up."

"It was us who cleaned up your mess last time," Beejee said as he swiped at the grackle.

It squawked back, pecking at Beejee's gray head.

"This is true," Cali said. She shimmered between the two familiars and shooed them away from each other. "And, anyway, we're handling it. For the most part."

Sediri scoffed. She pulled the strap of her black leather bag over her shoulder and dropped it on the table with a loud smacking sound. "Well, I come with supplies," she said, seemingly conceding her case. She rummaged through the bag, pulling books, and sparkling glass jars, and dried plants free. "Verol sent a bee for me," she said, looking up at last, with both hands full.

"A bee?" Lohrna asked from her space on the floor where she had still been busy decorating.

Sella was about to answer that it was an old tradition, a spell that could be used to transmit messages, though not a real bee, but Sediri went on as if she hadn't heard Lohrna at all.

"Apparently the military here has set their sights on the witches?"

Cali recoiled.

"The detective, mostly," Sella corrected.

"That's *worse*, Sella." Sediri crossed the shop and deposited her goods along the counter, lining them up carefully. "Please tell me you understand why that's worse, Sella."

Cali cut in, "Poem, the detective, is following any lead. We can't exactly fault him. The military is distrustful, yes, but we can take care of this. We *have* been taking care of this."

Sediri paused her work. She studied Cali carefully. "And have you given any thought on where you'll be staying?"

Cali pulled back as if she had been struck. "What do you mean?"

Sediri continued to organize her stash. "Well, I'm back now. Where will you folks be going?" She placed a single hand on her hip.

Her familiar hopped over to her with a few low chirping sounds.

She looked at him, then at Beejee with a sneer. "Unbelieveable," she said. She threw her hands up. "There's a hotel just down the road, I have arranged for you to get the largest room. By no small expense of my own." She looked at all of them, then shook her head. "No, no, please, don't everyone fall over themselves with gratitude."

Sella sighed. She leaned across the counter. "Sediri, you just got back, scolded us for how we've been handling a murder investigation, and are kicking us out... from what I can tell, *immediately*."

Sediri waved her hand. "Immediately, so dramatic. Of course, you'll have time to pack your things and change my sheets."

Sella deflated.

"You know," Lohrna called from the floor, still painting away. "I think we'll have better luck staying on the at least somewhat good side of these folks and the military if we're a little bit less..."

Both Sediri and Sella looked at her, waiting.

Lohrna finished the last petal of a purple flower. "... yourselves."

The witches exchanged a side glance at each other.

Cali raised a brow. "She has a point."

TWENTY-ONE

Sella, the Elemental Witch

"I CANNOT BELIEVE she is kicking us out after everything we've done for her," Beejee grumbled loudly as the group walked down the street, bags in hand.

Lohrna adjusted the bag across her shoulder. "Well," she said with a smile, "maybe we can look at this as an adventure? I've never stayed in a hotel before."

Cali laughed. "That's sweet."

"It is not," Beejee shot back.

Sella's gaze tilted up at the little two story building at the end of the street. "It's certainly going to be an adventure," she said quietly. "I assume the soldiers and the detective are also staying here."

"Too close for anything good to happen," Beejee said.

Cali's image flickered, just slightly.

Sella did her best to smile kindly, but she knew in her gut that she was failing Cali. Being close to family, who she couldn't talk to, and who probably didn't even know she was dead, was an unimaginable situation for her to be in. Sella felt helpless to make things right.

"Why don't you go see if Verol needs any help?" Sella suggested as they approached the large red door.

Cali smiled back, but lines on her forehead deepened. "You don't need to do that," she whispered. She looked at the red door and her expression shifted, turning neutral, then excited quickly. "This could be fun. I can haunt Amirisyali. Move her hair bands around to places she will least suspect. Be an annoying little sister again."

Beejee looked up at her. The tip of his tail flicked. "And while you're at it, sneak into Tate and Motet's room. Maybe you'll overhear something."

Cali raised a finger. "Yes, good idea."

Lohrna nudged at Beejee with her booted foot. "Don't give her an assignment," she scolded. "Come on, we'll make the spell to get Baz's temporary ghost to talk, and the whole thing will be solved. Easy."

"I don't know if you've noticed," Beejee said as they walked into the small lobby, "but nothing is ever easy for us."

The room was empty but for a little booth surrounded by small, light green plants, each with its one unique leaf pattern, though all stayed low to the pot and appeared pointed at the ends. Inside, a young man sat with his head in his hand, looking glum and bored.

Lohrna bounded up to him. "Hi!" She stuck her hand out to him and he took it with a hesitant shake.

"You must be the ones who booked the big room," he said as he let go of Lohrna's hand and rummaged below the booth. "Honestly, I never knew this place could get so busy," he mumbled under his breath.

"The big room?" Sella asked. "We haven't booked anything yet."

The man looked up, an old looking key hung from a gold chain in his hand. "Oh," he said. "The other witch booked it for you. The one with the horns?"

Sella and Lohrna exchanged a glance. Sella had been certain that Sediri was joking about getting them 'the big room'. She felt a little guilty for not thanking her now. While they were being kicked out, this seemed like the best in an uncomfortable situation. At least, for them.

"Yes," the man said, jotting something down in his little book on the wood counter. "Even bought out the officer in the room. She was *not* too happy with that." He looked up with a friendly smile and handed Lohrna the key. "Here we go. You are in the second floor room, number 3. Just go up those stairs and you'll see it."

THE ROOM WAS dark as the sun set on the other side of the building. The little window provided a dull, dim ray of light along the floor, the rest of the room was in shadow.

"I can't see anything," Lohrna complained. She fumbled with the door, trying to get it open wider.

Sella waved her hand and a warm glow of little floating fires filled the room with a small crackle sound.

"Now that's homey," Cali mused to herself.

"Glad you're enjoying the extra space," Amiri said, her voice suddenly too close.

Lohrna jumped, leaping back with her hand over her chest. "Tides!" she cried through a gasping breath.

Sella smiled. She had grown accustomed to Cali popping out of thin air. A memory flashed through her mind where once Cali told Sella that her family used to say they ought to put a bell on her. Even in life, she had a way of showing up out of nowhere. Clearly, it was a family trait.

"I'm sorry we took your room," Sella said sincerely.

"I still think it's bad practice on the hotel's part," Amiri said, folding her arms and widening her stance. "We would never be treated like this in a bigger town."

Cali stood beside her sister. She smiled brightly and pointed. "Watch this!" she said.

Sella's eyes widened.

Cali bit her bottom lip and as hard as she could, she shoved her sister with both hands.

Amiri's shoulder twitched. She seemed otherwise unfazed.

Cali looked up at her sister with a pout.

Sella's lips pulled tightly into a thin line to try to keep herself from laughing.

Cali folded her arms in much the same way that her sister did. "It's not funny," she said, though her face betrayed her. "I'm trying to do my little sister duties."

Sella looked up at the ceiling, doing her best to avoid laughing.

Amiri frowned at her. "Well," the soldier said, "I hope you go to bed early. We are all morning risers here."

Sella blinked slowly. "Is there an oven in the room by chance?"

Amiri 's expression shifted. "No," she said as if she couldn't believe she was being asked at all.

"Then it should be no problem," Lohrna, thankfully, cut in. "Sella's a late night baker. If we don't have that, you should be sleeping soundly."

Amiri only nodded curtly back and slipped past Sella to her new room. She glanced back at them for a moment, then disappeared behind the door.

THE ROOM WAS LARGER than Sella expected. Two small beds were strangely placed in an L shape with a large table in the middle and four tall chairs. A shelf of candles lined the high wall and multiple thick rugs covered the wood floor in shades of green and gold.

Lohrna pushed her small bed to the far wall so she could rest her head against the wall they shared with Amiri's new room. She closed her eyes and sighed gently. "What a day," she said.

Sella sat on her own bed, watching Beejee slink around the perimeter of the room, his little nose twitching as he went. "I feel kind of bad about taking this room," she said.

"Don't," Cali said as she lay beside Sella, her head resting in the witch's lap. She looked up at her with bright green eyes, all the more vibrant among the room's textiles.

She reached a hand for Sella's and their fingers laced slowly. "She was always taking my things as a kid." She blinked, her brows furrowed. "Or was it my brother?"

Sella felt a jolt of pain in her gut at the uncertainty in Cali's voice. Memory was strange like that, she thought. It was easy to fill in the gaps with things that were happening in the present. Easy to justify your own past story as your current one unfolded. And no matter how she tried to hold her own, as years went on, things began to distort and slip away.

Cali smiled nonetheless and Sella felt herself do the same.

Memory wasn't all they had.

Beejee curled up at the foot of Lohrna's bed, having thoroughly checked the room to his satisfaction.

Little shadows flickered over their faces, and across the clay walls. And from her position on her new bed, Sella could see the sky full of starlight and contentment pushed aside anything else that had tried to take root in her heart.

They also had right now.

It was flawed and beautiful and even a little painful. But it was here. It was now. It was warm and safe. And nothing about tomorrow or yesterday could change that.

TWENTY-TWO

The Wyvern is a Menace

IN THE EARLY MORNING LIGHT, Sella squinted up to the roof of the hotel. Her hand hovered over her brow as she tried to see the exact position that the wyvern was in. For now, all she could definitely say was that its wings were folded around its body, and its tail was draped down the side of the building. Where its head was, she couldn't be sure.

She stood among the group of witches, and for the first time in a long time, she didn't feel like an outsider. The others clustered close to her, no one seemingly afraid of her or worried that she was going to hurt them. Her chest expanded with a long inhale as she savored the feeling of belonging.

On the roof, the wyvern let out a low growl and all the good she felt evaporated as worry took root in her core.

"How long has he been up there?" Lohrna asked.

"All morning," Verol said, her hands on her hips.

"Is he causing any damage?" Lohrna mimicked her pose and tilted her head to one side.

"That's the thing," Verol said. "We don't know, but the hotel proprietor is unhappy with it."

Lazil leaned in. "I do think the weight of the thing might end up damaging the roof. On the next rain, it could cause leaking."

Cali shrugged. "They're lighter than you think," she said. "Powerful, but not exactly strong."

Sediri stroked her grackle's beak as it perched on her shoulder. "Like a bird," she offered.

Cali nodded. "A really, really big, scaly eagle. With teeth. That breathes fire sometimes."

"Have we tried throwing rocks at it?" Beejee asked.

Lohrna and Verol both looked at him with mouths hung open.

"What?" the cat protested.

Lazil scratched the back of her head. "I mean…?"

"We're not throwing rocks at it. It's napping!" Lohrna said, a harsh whisper as if her words would wake the creature, like it was a sleeping baby and not a massive monster.

Sella raised a brow.

"I just don't see why we're in charge of this menace," Beejee went on. "Where are its masters?"

"Well, its master is dead." Cali pointed to the wyvern. "That's Lucanairi. You can tell by the coloring."

Beejee scoffed. "The soldiers are still off doing oceans know what. They should be here handling this."

"I agree," Lazil said.

Sediri shifted her weight, long hair fell over her shoulder and her familiar flapped his wings in protest. "Well, Sella?"

Sella's eyes widened. "Well what?"

"What are you going to do about it?"

"Why me?"

Sediri waved a hand at her. "I admit, begrudgingly, that you are the most powerful one here. You don't even use a wand. You must know what to do."

Lohrna laughed, cutting the tension with her good nature once again. "Yes, but you're asking Sella to make a decision."

Sella's brows furrowed in feigned offense, though part of her felt a sting as the truth in her friend's words burrowed into her heart. "I can make decisions. Eventually. I'm just… not sure about this one."

Cali slipped a hand into Sella's.

"Wait," Verol said. "You don't use a wand?"

Sediri's smile was almost wicked. "She doesn't. Don't tell me those twigs she carries around have fooled you."

Verol and Lazil exchanged glances.

"You can do this," Cali whispered.

Sella squeezed Cal's hand. She wasn't so sure she could do anything about a situation like this. She let go at last and tucked her hair behind her ears. "Does anyone know a bug summoning spell? We could lure him down with a snack."

"That would work on me," Lohrna said. "The snack, not the bugs."

Verol raised her wand. "I could try?"

Sediri's eyes narrowed. "You're a hedge witch," she said. "What will you do? Sprout grass beneath our feet and wait for the insects to appear?"

Verol glared at Sediri for a moment. She held her head higher. "What's the other side of life and growth? I can work with death and decay too."

Sediri's shoulders broadened as she met Verol's stare. At last, the two of them both curled the side of their lips up in a small grin, reaching some quick and silent truce. Though if it was from admiration or fear of aggression, Sella couldn't be sure.

"You did find the necromancy spell," Sediri finally conceded. Her smile grew.

Verol threw her hands up, as though they had this discussion over and over again. "It's *not* a necromancy spell! And Lazil found it."

Lazil shrugged. "Only because your intuition told me where to look."

Lohrna leaned in. "Wait," she said, "Lazil, you found the spell to bring back the ghost?"

"Last night," she said with a nod.

Beejee's ear flicked. He looked behind him. "No need for decay magic," he said. "And put your wand away."

At Verol's side, her little cat meowed at him.

The group turned to see the three soldiers coming down the road, each wearing a different expression showing shades of varying degrees of unhappiness from Tate's concerned furrow to Amiri's angry snarl. She quickened her pace, leaving the others to scramble to keep up.

"What are you doing?" Amiri demanded. Her eyes darted from the wyvern to the wand in Verol's hand. "Harming a wyvern is punishable by–"

"No one was going to hurt Lucanairi," Sella said, her hands raised innocently. She motioned for Verol to lower her wand, now pointed weakly at the soldiers. "He's causing damage to this building, you were nowhere to be found. We were going to summon him a lure."

Amiri cocked her head. "The law dictates that they are not liable for any damage. You have no right to raise your weapons against him."

Sella shook her head. "A wand is not a weapon, Amiri."

"It doesn't matter if the law is on your side," Verol growled through gritted teeth, knuckles straining under her skin as she clutched her wand. "You have the moral obligation to do right by us when you come to our home. You are here to protect *us* or have you forgotten?"

Cali moved to stand between the witches and her sister. "Stop it," she whispered, her hair waved around her arms in a whirlwind of her own creation.

Sella and Beejee lurched to her side. She had been able to keep the peace between Cali and the witches so far. But it was their job to banish unhappy spirits. Even if none of them knew the spell to do so, she couldn't risk straining the few relationships Cali had cultivated in her death. "You're here now," she told Amiri. "Help us get him free from the roof. That's all we're asking for."

Amiri's eyes swept over Sella from head to foot in a

slow, careful motion. "Tell them to put their weapons away," she said.

Beejee hissed but Sella simply nodded to the witches.

Verol's grip loosened. She stuffed her wand in her sleeve.

"And you," Amiri said. "Hands behind your back."

Sella flinched. "Me?"

"I saw what you can do," Amiri said, so quiet Sella was almost unsure she heard her at all.

"Sella, don't!" Cali said.

Sella cast a gentle smile at Cali. She slowly put her hands behind her back, lacing her fingers together. She did her best to stand tall. "It's going to be alright," she said. To Cali, to Beejee, to herself…

Lohrna watched the scene with an agitated unease, nearly bouncing as her body swayed. "Well then?" she gestured from the soldiers to the wyvern. "They did what you asked. Help us."

Motet and Tate moved to stand by Amiri's side. She smiled, then cupped her hands around her mouth. She shouted a few commands in a language Sella didn't recognize, and the wyvern's tail flicked.

A long pause followed and Sella's skin began to prickle with sweat. The sun was too warm. The ground beneath her, too loose as the wind picked up. Sand between the travertine pavers raked across the road and the wyvern's wings began to beat.

Lucanairi growled, then stood on his long legs. He looked down at the soldiers and snarled, then took off into the clear blue sky.

Amiri's attention was back on the witches in an instant. Her green eyes were fierce in the morning light. "Do not raise your wands to a wyvern again," she warned. "I will excuse your ignorance this time. It will not happen again." She turned on her heel and motioned for Tate and Motet to follow.

"Don't be such a snake!" Cali called after her.

Amiri flinched. She turned over her shoulder for just a moment before she kept walking down the road and out of sight.

Lohrna let out a heavy sigh. She bent down and rested her hands on her knees as though she had just run a very long way. "I did not enjoy that," she huffed out.

Verol's hands were still clenched tight. She growled between gritted teeth. "I'm tired of them coming in here like they… like they…" Her chest rose and fell rapidly, her breath releasing in quick huffs.

Sella hurried to her side. "Not here," she whispered as she held Verol's elbows gently in her hands. She bent down to catch her eyes but Verol's gaze was fixed to the ground, a deep set of wrinkles formed between her brows. "Come with me," she said. She looked up to the other witches, then motioned for them to follow. "Let's go to the shop," she ordered. "Quickly. Come on, Verol. Walk with us."

Verol nodded, but her eyes didn't move, her feet were planted.

Lohrna placed a hand on Sella's back. She nodded to Sella to get walking, then wrapped her own arm in the crook of Verol's elbow. She pulled the hedge witch forward with steady, small steps. "You're safe," she whispered. "Come on, Sella will make you something perfect at the shop."

Verol nodded, letting herself be led down the road.

Sella's heart ached as she headed up the group with Cali at her side. "We just need to solve this case," she said quietly. "And then we can all focus on what we need…" A need to heal, to be brave, to grow, to speak… So many needs.

Right now, what she needed to do was to make a blend to satisfy at least one of them. A cozy blend to feel safe.

TWENTY-THREE

Yes, No, No Maybes

THE SUN WAS low in the sky as Sella bit her lip as she stared at the spell. It could bring back a ghost for three questions. But it could only answer in an agreement or a disagreement.

"A simple 'yes' or a 'no'," Verol guessed.

But Sella was tired of trying to figure things out in riddles or within strange parameters. She sighed.

"We'll just have to get clever," Cali said. "Like we did with the pixie last year."

Sella rubbed the bridge of her nose. "Don't remind me," she grumbled.

"Unfortunately, this may be our best chance at solving this unless some other clues fall from the sky," Lazil said. "And you're the best equipped to make it."

Don't tell them about 'The Incident', a voice in Sella's head echoed through her mind. She shook it away before she could linger on it. Back home, no one would let her live down the time she gave the town spots during a spell gone wrong. This would be different. Sella was sure of it.

The group of witches, their familiars, and Lohrna, were crowded around the table in the room above the potion shop. Sella couldn't help but feel a little displaced there now. It had been her temporary home for long enough that it now felt like everyone else was trespassing on her space, though Sediri had heavily changed the decor in her short time back, leaving no trace of Sella or Lohrna or even Beejee.

It had been swept clean of all fur. New rugs covered the wooden floors, and she had hung up woven art along the walls. A pair of men's boots waited at the door for her partner to return and take up even more of the space. He was still on his travels with family, though Sediri had cut her vacation short.

Sella thought it wasn't especially chivalrous of him to leave her on her own, but something about the way Sediri carried herself made her suspect that she liked it that way. At least, she hadn't complained about his absence yet.

Sella pulled her mind back to the task ahead of them: the creation of the spell to hopefully put this whole thing to rest once and for all. Then, she'd be able to focus on finding the spell for Cali. On remaking her mother's wand. On just anything other than a murder.

For once.

"It's going to be a bit strange for you all to be here watching me do this," Sella said. She looked at each of the ingredients on the table, thankful, at least, that the spell was based in kitchen magic despite it being very old, and of a different culture than her own.

"You'll get over it," Sediri said bluntly. "We're here for backup. Yes, you're capable, but you're also wandless."

A wandless menace, Sediri had once called her. The memory ignited a spark in Sella's chest. She could do this. She picked up the translated spell, a copy Lazil had written neatly on a new parchment.

She took a deep breath, and got to work.

THE TAVERN WAS CLOSED, much to the dismay of Echori and Rae, who grumbled loudly at the door when Verol shut it gently in their faces. None of the witches were sure if the spell would work, or in what capacity, and Beejee recommended they have a larger space than the room above the shop, just in case.

"Every time *she's* around, the spells backfire," Beejee had warned with his eyes fixed on Lohrna.

And it was true, Lohrna and Sella had gotten into a fair bit of messes in their youth when they were trying to concoct spells together. A stink spell, a spell that gave everyone spots... Both were temporary. And if Sella was being honest, neither had been Lohrna's fault. All the blame fell on Sella's inexperience and immature, unearned confidence.

She has grown out of that quickly. Now, she was standing before the group with a humbled sense of self. She was capable but cautious.

Poem and the witches, their familiars, and Lohrna

were all gathered around the counter watching Sella as she drank the potion quickly.

She held the parchment with the translated words carefully and spoke them aloud, trying her best to get the pronunciation of Baz's name correct. She looked up, first to Cali, who smiled and shrugged back, and then to the rest of the group.

"Does anyone see a ghost…?" Sella asked.

Cali waved.

"Not you," Beejee said, though there was kindness in his tone. His focus turned to Lohrna. "At least we aren't covered in stripes."

Lohrna's eyes narrowed at him though her smile was wide. She gestured at him and his dark gray stripes.

"No one else, then," he said and thrust his head the other way.

Sella looked around them. "Why didn't it work? Did I say his name wrong?"

Cali shook her head. "I don't think so. Maybe we got an ingredient misproportioned?"

Poem shifted his feet, his hands casually in the pockets of his oversized pants. His gaze moved from Sella to the other witches. "Well?"

Sella's fingers turned cold. Despite the warmth outside, she felt as though she had slowly begun to sink into the damp earth. She looked down at her hands. "I don't know," she said. "I don't know…"

Lazil scratched behind her ear. "Perhaps you do need a wand? You'd be more powerful with one."

Poem raised a brow. "You don't use a wand? That's unusual, isn't it?"

Sella rubbed her arms, trying to warm herself.

"Only to some," Lohrna said quickly.

She was right, technically. In Marra, their home, no one thought anything of Sella and her ability to use magic without it. Though, that was simply a matter of ignorance. Still, Sella was grateful that Lohrna had stepped it.

Poem looked at each of them in turn. "Can she not borrow one?"

Each witch flinched as though she had been deeply insulted.

"No," they said in unison.

Poem sighed. "Then one of you should perform the spell."

Sediri put a hand on her hip. She rolled her eyes. "I *could* try," she said. "But I begrudgingly admit I don't think it would work."

"Or… We could try to repair my mother's wand," Sella suggested. She fished the spell from her pocket, the one she had been carrying since she found the way to open it in ocean water. "I just don't know enough of this kind of magic to do it. I haven't wanted to risk trying and failing, damaging it further…"

Poem shifted, then shrugged as though none of this was in the least bit interesting. "Send for me when you are able to try this again," he said. "I will need to be there when we interrogate the general."

Sella sighed as Poem left the tavern, the door shutting behind him with a definitive slam.

Cali rested her head in her hand. "Picking out thorns when we're trapped in the bush..." She sounded disappointed.

Sediri raised a brow at Sella but Verol simply nodded.

"So it would seem," the hedge witch said. "Well, let's make the people's day and open up. We'll try fixing up the wand tonight. After we've had some rest." Her eyes shifted to Sella, her shoulders still curled in on herself. "That means you."

Sella wanted to cry, or scream. She wasn't sure. But the frustration vanished when she felt Beejee's fur along her calf. He nudged into her with affection and grace. She scooped him up and felt the small vibrations of his purr deep within her chest.

"I could use a nap too," Lohrna said with a yawn. "I didn't even do anything. Come on, friends. Let's leave the humans to their day."

IT WAS WELL into the night when Verol held the pieces of the broken wand in her hands as though it were a delicate bird she was afraid of crushing with the slightest pressure. The tips of her fingers curled over the shards protectively as her eyes darted across the spell scroll that Sella had given her.

"I can see why you'd have trouble doing this spell on your own," she said at last. Her gaze landed back on the wand and her brows furrowed at the splinters. "This is a powerful wand. I can feel the forcefulness with which you broke it." She looked back up at Sella and smiled gently. "It *is* nearly gone," she said. "But not yet. You would probably need me to repair it. Or someone like me."

Lohrna nudged Verol with her shoulder. "A hedge-witch who balances life and death, sure. But there's only one you."

Verol smiled back. "A friend," she confirmed. "Someone who knows you. Spells dealing with repair and rebirth are like that."

Beejee's ear twitched and Sella understood. Someone who knew her. As much as she wanted to be known by the witches here, she still felt like a stranger. She had kept everyone separate from herself, seen them as something she wasn't. Even now that the other witches had rallied behind her in the face of a threat, she still didn't feel like a real witch. Like she really belonged.

Beejee pressed his head against her calf, slinked his body along her leg until his tail wrapped around her. He looked up and she smiled at him, though a tear in her eye stung.

"I'll do my best to revive this," Verol said at last, as if she understood. "But I think I will need your help." She looked at Lohrna. "You too."

"Me?"

"Her?" Beejee's voice overlapped Lohrna's.

Verol nodded. She motioned for Lohrna and Sella to come closer as she extended her own wand in her other hand. "You may not be a witch, but I suspect having you close will help. Part of bringing something magic back is giving it a reason *to be* back."

Lohrna's expression shifted to confusion. She looked at Beejee but he only nodded in return as if it all made perfect sense. He had given her his permission to come close as a spell was cast. Sella wondered if Lohrna felt honored, or frightened.

"Alright," Lohrna said slowly, approaching the group with careful steps.

It seemed, Sella thought, that she felt both in equal parts.

"Hands," Verol ordered as she closed her eyes.

Sella and Lohrna each reached a hand out to the broken wand.

"You too," Verol said with eyes still shut.

Sella reached out for Cali, who took her hand with a hesitant hum.

A warmth spread through them as Verol whispered the words to the ancient spell to fix broken things.

TWENTY-FOUR

The Silver in the Cracks

THE WAND WAS JUST as she remembered it and yet…

Sella turned it over in her hand, her fingers running the length of the smooth wood gently. The last time she held it, she snapped it, poured all her energy into breaking it into pieces. She threw it on the wet grass to rot with the rest of a long forgotten space so that no one could ever again use it for harm.

She had been angry and confused about why her mother had given it to someone else instead of her when she passed. Even now, it didn't really make sense to her, except that perhaps the trust between them had eroded faster than the magic within the wand ever could.

And yet, most of her memories with this wand had been warm, kind. Times spent watching her mother perform magic of all kinds in the comfort of their home. A place where despite the rain outside, it always appeared sunny inside.

Sella turned it over again. She studied the shattered place where she had snapped it in two. It was whole now, a shimmer of silver almost hidden in the dark grain where it had fused together again.

She looked at Verol and tears fell from her eyes before she even understood what she felt inside. Overwhelm, gratitude, confusion… "Thank you," she whispered as Cali and Lohrna each placed a hand on her back.

Verol smiled at her. "You're welcome," she said, her voice tired. "Repairing broken things doesn't come easily. Thank you all for the help."

Her familiar leaped onto the counter beside her and meowed loudly.

Beejee nudged Sella with his head again. "Time to go," he said.

Sella nodded and wiped the tears from her face as best she could with the back of her hand. "We'll let you rest."

"We'll try the other spell again soon," Verol said. "When we gather all the ingredients again."

LOHRNA NEARLY BOUNDED down the street ahead of Sella and Cali. Beejee trotted alongside her. The two seemed to be enthralled in each other's conversation, but Sella merely held her wand in both hands and trailed behind them, lost in her own thoughts.

Holding the wand now, one she thought at first was lost, then corrupted, broken, and now repaired with the help of a magic so powerful that even she did not under-stand it... felt almost anticlimactic. She was happy. She thought she was, at least. But also, numb.

Cali tilted her body to catch Sella's eyes. She smiled. "You lost?"

Sella blinked, then stuffed the wand into her pocket. "Have a map?"

Cali's smile brightened. She looked ahead to the other. "I'm familiar with these lands. I'll show you the way."

Another sting of salt burned in Sella's eyes. She looked up, folding her hands behind her back to stretch casually as they walked. The emotions and thoughts running through her were too complex to hold. But she didn't want anyone else to carry them. "What should I do with it first?" Sella asked with a half smile to hide her growing turbulence.

They turned the corner to see the hotel, nestled among the other buildings, and free of any giant, sleeping beasts.

"Is there a spell to create a fireplace that doesn't get too hot?" Cali asked. "I miss having our cozy nights together."

"A fire that doesn't get hot, yes," Sella said. "Creating a whole fireplace? Probably not. But I'll keep searching."

"Ooo! How about one to talk to wyverns!"

Sella raised a brow. "That feels possible." And it did. If witches and wyverns used to bond, if riders could control wyvern fire, even if only for a moment, then... wouldn't it be possible?

It would certainly make solving the murder easier if they could simply ask the wyverns for their alibis.

For now, however, Sella was content to simply be among her friends as they found their way to their safe little space in the upstairs rented room. She flicked her wrist instinctively and the little fires lit overhead, warming the space in a friendly glow.

"Can you make biscuits with the wand?" Lohrna asked as she flung herself onto the bed that she had pushed up against the far wall. She hung one hand over the edge and yawned loudly. "Because I'm starving and I really don't want to go to the market if we don't have to."

"Since when do you not want to go out?" Beejee asked, taking a curled up position on Sella's bed.

"Tomorrow's the full moon," Lohrna said. She opened one eye to look at Beejee. "And I think my help might've taken it out of me. Is this how you always feel after doing spellwork?"

"Oh, Verol just wanted you to feel included," Beejee said. The tip of his tail flicked and Sella knew he was lying. Lohrna and Cali may not be witches, but there was something more profound than magic about bringing back a broken, *mostly* dead thing that none of them understood.

"I'll go get us something to eat," Sella said, ignoring Beejee for now.

"I'll go, too." Cali appeared at her side in a swirling mist.

"Bring back lots of food," Lohrna called as Sella stepped back through the door. "*Lots*, Sella."

"Lots of food, got it."

"Sella. A LOT."

Sella laughed. "A lot. Right," she said and closed the door gently, leaving her friend and familiar to lounge and chat.

THE NIGHT SKY WAS CLEAR, filled from horizon to horizon with brilliant stars. The nearly full moon illuminated the market with a pale glow.

It was busy, as it usually seemed to be.

As Sella and Cali weaved their way through the people, she still marveled at how alive the town came at night. It made sense, though. In Marra, the night brought mist and chill, and the occasional pixie. Here, with the sun's rays no longer touching skin, the night was much more tolerable and there were no annoying little flying pixies trying to cause mischief or steal things.

Sella stopped at different vendors, through Cali's guidance, to load up her bag with foods and treats. She bought strange looking fruit that Cali insisted were delicious, despite their spikey outsides, and crispy dried meat that the ghost warned were spicy but addicting.

They maneuvered to the edges of the market once Sella's bag was sufficiently stuffed and stopped to look back, checking that they hadn't missed anything from the outside view.

"Do you think Lohrna will be terribly mad if we stay out just a little longer?" Cali asked.

Sella looked down at her bag. Nothing in it would spoil soon. She smiled at Cali. "Honestly? She and Beejee are probably already asleep."

Cali's hand slipped in Sella's. "Let's stay here for a moment, then," she said, pointing to a small alcove in the outer wall on the outskirts of the market.

Sella let Cali lead the way, though her pull was hardly more than a suggestion. The ghost was semi-translucent in the torchlight. A starfilled calm settled over the night market even as it got busier and sitting in their little nook, watching the crowd, Sella felt as though she was miles away from it all.

People, their faces illuminated in warm firelight, laughed and hugged, they bought and sold, moved and waited, and, as Sella noticed, *lived*.

She frowned.

"How are you feeling?" Cali asked after a moment. "Happy to have your mother's wand?"

Sella's mouth twitched. But she couldn't quite smile. "I…" Sella stopped. She looked down at her hands, at Cali's, cold and only half there resting on her own. "How are you? With your sister being here…"

Cali shook her head. "You're trying to change the subject."

Sella's eyes softened. She squeezed Cali's hand and her fingers passed through. "No," she said. "I really feel that we haven't had the time and space to talk about it. I want to know how you are, what you're feeling—"

"I hate it," Cali cut her off. Her hand withdrew, wrapping around her own torso quickly as if she was going to be sick. "I hate seeing her here. I left this place because I wanted to be away. And I don't know if any of my family even know I'm... dead. Maybe Rorin had the decency to tell them, but I doubt it."

Sella looked down at the ground.

Rorin, Cali's ex-boyfriend, had come to Marra shortly after her death when he believed that Cali had written him a letter asking for his help. It had been a ploy, though Sella thought a not terribly clever one, by Cali's killer to frame him for her death. He arrived in Marra, camped in the woods, acted incredibly guilty, worked only in his self interest and then left as quickly as he had come once his name was cleared.

Cali has a point.

It was unlikely he had told her family. Especially since Cali hadn't spoken to any of them in years.

"I can't imagine what you're feeling," Sella said at last.

Cali shook her head. "Most of the time, I don't mind so much. Being dead, that is. I have a life still. I have you. And Lohrna on the full moons. Beejee and Koukie... But seeing her here is a reminder that I'm still not *alive*. I don't get to yell and be mad at my family. I don't get to tell them I'm better off without them or that I still love them, either. It's almost like I'm forced to make peace and I don't want to. Is that silly?"

"Not at all," Sella said. "None of that is."

Cali leaned back, her head rested on the clay building

behind them. "When you find the spell to let me talk, I'll be sure to give Amiri a stern talking to."

Sella laughed before she could catch it in her throat. She covered her mouth with her hand quickly.

Cali glared at her, though her expression was playful. "What?" she said. "I can give stern talkings to. You don't know."

Sella nodded. "Right," she said through her fingers. "I know you can." She wanted to add that the most important thing was that Cali also had every right to. She wanted to tell her that no matter what, she'd work hard to get the spell Cali needed and that she'd support her in whatever she decided to do with her newfound ability. That she wasn't going to stop until she got it. That she loved her—

A scream broke Sella's thoughts. It cut through the crisp air, drowning out the noise of the market.

Sella and Cali shot up quickly.

A fire ignited in Sella's hand but Cali covered it quickly with her own. She shook her head, eyes wide.

"Your wand," the ghost whispered.

Sella nodded and pulled the wand from her pocket as the screaming grew, many voices now joining as one.

"Go check on Lohrna," Sella said as she hurried toward the crowd.

Cali shimmered from her periphery as more people joined the huddle at the farthest side of the market. A few pointed down the alley as Sella approached. From here, she could see the source of their panic.

Massive flames shot up into the air, engulfing several wooden booths and spreading fast.

Sella's heart beat loudly in her ears, her eyes grew wider, taking it all in. Her gaze searched the flames for signs that anyone had been hurt or was trapped, but it was too bright to tell.

Ahead, she saw Lazil's silhouette, her familiar perched along her neck. She was holding something in her hands, but what, Sella couldn't see.

She turned back, but the crowd was even farther now, and Cali was gone.

Sella's jaw hardened and she ran to Lazil's side, the flames hot on her skin as she approached. Now, as she stood beside Lazil, she could see the two rods in the other witch's hands, moving about in her loose grip.

"Know any spells to put out fires?" Lazil asked with a half smile, though her eyes betrayed her fear.

Sella bit her lip. She looked into the fire. She could create fire, but could not control it. That has always been her downfall, the emotional burst and then the burns...

In the flames, Sella thought she saw the tips of wings beating, a wall of heat blasted forward toward them. She squinted into the brightly burning flames. A wyvern was lost in there. Stuck and frantic. Or perhaps, the source of the chaos.

"A wyvern is there," she breathed out at last. She gestured to the rods in Lazil's hand and louder asked, "A spell?"

"I'm looking for water," Lazil explained quickly. "If I can find it, I can use it."

Sella lifted her hand, wand ready. Her mind was frenzied with trying to recall any spell she knew. But all she could come up with was a recipe for calm, a recipe for self love, recipes… recipes… She growled, furious at herself.

"Ah!" Lazil nearly jumped forward. "Found you," she whispered as her rods crossed over themselves. She looked back at Sella and pointed at the ground. "Water!"

Sella angled her wand at the ground and before she could recall where she knew the spell, she spoke the words for destruction.

The ground quaked beneath them, splitting clay and cracking dirt down deeper and deeper until she could no longer see the bottom in the dark night.

"Perfect!" Lazil held her hand high, summoning the water from deep within the earth. She whispered words Sella did not know as water quickly rose from the ground, shooting up in a brilliant burst.

It began to rain down on the fire, a sizzling sound filled the air and cooled them instantly.

As quickly as it had begun, the fire was gone but the market was in ruins. Droplets shimmered in the silver glow of the moon as black smoke billowed from the ash and debris.

The wyvern crouched down among the rubble, snarling a low growl with exposed sharp teeth. Sella could not hear the rumble among the gasps and cries of the people behind her, but she saw the flash of yellow teeth and the snapping of jaws. She narrowed her eyes, trying to see what the wyvern was doing in the dark.

It flapped one wing, revealing the huddled body of the old meat seller, Cosas. He looked up from his defensive position in a slow, steady movement, lowering his arms that he had wrapped around his head.

The wyvern's long neck curled back, nudging Cosas gently with its snout.

Lazil cast Sella a quick glance, then rushed to their side with Sella close behind.

TWENTY-FIVE

The Wing and the Cook

THE NIGHT MARKET crowd that had been positioned far from the wreckage was now all gathered around the wyvern, who Sella now recognized as Lucanairi by his coloring and fierceness with which he eyed anyone who got too close. One wing was still positioned around Cosas, though if it was for protection or possessiveness, Sella couldn't discern.

She held out an arm, preventing Lazil and her familiar from stepping any closer.

Lazil raised a brow but Sella silently shook her head.

The wyvern was dangerous, even if Lazil didn't seem to think so.

Still, he looked at her with eyes wider than she had ever seen them before. As if, Sella thought, he was frightened. Or, perhaps, just trying to see better in the low light. She positioned herself in front of Lazil.

Frightened things could do a terrible amount of damage and his teeth and claws were sharp.

After a quiet moment, he snorted as Cosas' hand reached out to the wyvern's neck. His scales glistened in the moonlight as his muscles rippled under the human's touch.

Sella's shoulders relaxed. A long exhale released tension in her back as she watched with curiosity and relief.

It didn't last long.

"Stand back!" a voice called out into the night.

The crowd behind them parted and a sudden silence descended upon them as the military members strode up, casually, as though they were in no hurry. As though their wyvern wasn't in the middle of the wreckage of the square, guarding an old human man with low growling and barred teeth.

Amiri, with the others close behind her, stopped at the edge of the crowd. Her green eyes moved about each face, then to the wyvern, then to Sella. Her jaw tightened. "What happened here?" she demanded.

Sella let out a frustrated growl before she could stop herself. "Lucanairi–"

Amiri pointed to the massive crater in the earth between them. "What happened *here*?"

Sella winced. "Your wyvern–"

Amiri cut her off again, one hand raised to silence her. "You did this?"

Lazil crossed her arms. "A simple 'thank you' would suffice," she said. "Sella cracked the earth to get enough water to put out the fire that your wyvern *clearly* started."

She gestured back to the creature. "Cosastatelan is lucky to be alive."

Cosas, finally free of the wyvern's wing, stood taller. He rubbed his face with the back of one wrinkled hand. "The wyvern didn't start the fire," he said slowly. "Though, I think he might have exasperated it… But he saved me."

"It's true," another person in the crowd said. But who, Sella couldn't be sure. "It was the fire, it got out of hand."

"I must have used too much oil," Cosas said in a pained tone. "When it ignited the roof of my stand, the wyvern flew in. I don't even know from where."

"This wyvern doesn't have a master," Poem's voice was clear, cutting through the crowd.

Sella nearly jumped from his sudden appearance, but Poem didn't seem to notice her unease as he stepped forward. He went on, "Lucanairi needs firmer guidance."

"He has it," Amiri said quickly, one hand on her hip. She barked out a quick command and the wyvern grimaced, then stood on its thick legs, head bowed low. She said another, and after a quick snarl, his wings stretched out and with two powerful strokes, he took off, disappearing into the night sky. Amiri turned back to Poem with a half smile. "Do not question me," she warned, her voice low.

"How will we repair this?" a voice lamented from the crowd.

"Was anyone injured?" another inquired, worry heavy in their tone.

Sella took in a deep breath, the scent of smoke and

wood and sweat filled her in a sudden wave of dizziness as reality crashed in. The grip on her wand tightened. "Did everyone make it out?" Sella asked Cosas.

He nodded. "I was trapped behind my counter. Everyone in the aisle made it out, but if it wasn't for the wyvern, I don't think I would be here talking to you."

Sella looked back at the crowd, at their distressed expressions, all half in shadow. In her hand, the wand felt warm.

She was a kitchen witch. Certified, as Beejee liked to point out.

And she was an elemental witch, though she tried her best to hide it. She had worked hard over decades. Struggling and growing. She had traveled far from home and done her best to learn from every mistake as she went. She had banished ghosts, and saved one, too.

And here, now, as another witch looked up at her with worry in her eyes, and a soldier with disdain, and a crowd with hope, she knew that all of it had been for *something*.

Even if it wasn't much.

Her feet shifted, grounding herself to the earth beneath her. "I can fix this," she said, her voice strong and louder than the voices surrounding them. She looked back to Lazil with a warm smile, and then to Amiri. "I will fix this."

TWENTY-SIX

A Simple Sign Ought to Do the Trick

THE MORNING CAME SWIFTLY, the light of the sun had hardly crested the tops of the buildings when Sella felt the crushing weight of her promise on her chest. And Beejee.

He was nose to nose with her, his little paws pressing down on her collarbone. "Wake up. You have a lot to do. Let's go get coffee."

Sella blinked a few times, trying to clear the mist that lingered in her mind. She yawned, and pushed Beejee off of her gently. Perhaps it had all been a wild dream?

But as she pushed herself up from her bed, she saw the dark soot on her fingertips, found her wand on the pillow beside her, and Cali sitting at the foot of her bed with a wild smile.

Sella rubbed her eyes, her mouth stretched wide with another yawn. "Why are you so happy?" she asked, her voice still hoarse.

Cali leaned in, the bed shifted. "Because you are *amazing* and I love you."

Sella's eyes flew open and her cheeks warmed. "I… I love you too." It was always just as surprising to her, even a year later, that Cali spoke those words to her.

How lucky she felt every time.

Across the room, Lohrna rolled over in her bed. She flung one arm to hang over the side. "Coffee," she croaked with only one eye open. "Now."

Sella rolled her neck, trying to loosen the heaviness that settled in her muscles. The scuffs on the back of her hand as she stretched her arms out served as an unfriendly reminder that she had work to do. And she wasn't entirely sure how to do it.

Coffee would be a necessity today.

WITH A CERAMIC CUP stolen from the hotel lobby in one hand, and her wand in the other, Sella overlooked the destruction she had created upon the market square with a sense of dread draining the blood from her face.

In the light of the morning, she could see the damage done from the fire. Nearly an entire row of booths had been turned to ash and black splintered wood and before her, the massive hole in the ground threatened to swallow her whole.

At least the other vendors had all packed up their booths and wares long before she got there. The square was empty, save the ruins.

She glanced down into the dark and shivered. It was deep, though thankfully, not too wide. She sipped her coffee and considered how bad it would be to just put some wood over it with a sign that said 'Stay Clear' and leave it at that.

But as her motivation blend kicked in, she started to see the path ahead. Clearing out the ruined booths would be, relatively, easy. That was merely a matter of time and brute force. The hole, however, might take more time. She didn't know a spell to repair something so huge, and hauling dirt from the fields outside the town to fill it didn't appeal to her either.

She tapped her chin with her wand and Beejee looked up at her expectantly.

"I'm not sure yet," she said.

"Good morning," Verol called from the other end of the square. She waved on hand up high in a chipper greeting. Behind her, Lazil, Rae, and a dozen or so villagers that Sella didn't recognize followed along, with buckets, crates, and farming tools. "We came to help!"

Sella smiled and relief sighed out of her as they all approached with determined but compassionate expressions.

Verol leaned down over the hole just as Sella had before. "Wow..." she whistled. "That's one powerful spell." She looked back at Sella. "Would be pretty great if you knew the opposite one, wouldn't it?"

Sella took another long sip. "It would," she said.

"No chance of doing this the easy way, then?" Lazil asked. "We can't magic our way to a clean space?"

Sella shook her head. "I'm afraid the cleaning part will be just manual labor," she said. "It's this hole that I think we can..." she paused, trying to find the right words, "...well, 'magic our way out of'."

Rae waved at the group to disburse. "Let's get to work," she said, authority and clarity in her tone that set the rest of them off to begin filling their wooden crates and buckets with debris.

"I better make it look good," Lazil said with a wink and set off to the group.

At her feet, Verol's familiar meowed.

Verol shrugged. "It could work," she said. She looked up at Sella. "Do you think we could work together on this? I know a spell to accelerate back growth after fires. If we fill this with the ashes, I think I'd be able to create a little garden here, if you help. Plus, Lazil can help water it."

"Of course," Sella said. "That's a great idea."

Verol looked back at the others. "Well, I wouldn't call it a great idea. I've been meaning to set one up here for a while, the sun is in a good position in the summer with how these buildings face..." She looked up at the two story buildings circling the open market. "But people have been hesitant to let me."

"They're going to think we planned this," Beejee said, though he was mostly joking.

"Quite the elaborate plan," Verol said with a laugh. "I'll let the others know."

SEDIRI SLID two cups of coffee across the bar and Beejee's eyes narrowed in response.

"What's in it?" he asked, suspicion heavy in his voice.

"Nothing but caffeine," Sediri shot back. She glanced at Sella for a moment as she sipped her drink, only to then busy herself behind the counter. "Since the signature drink still isn't finished," Sediri grumbled under her breath.

"You came back early," Beejee said.

Sediri tossed her head to one side dramatically, though still avoiding his gaze. "Yes, well every time I'm around you folks, someone ends up dead."

Beejee hissed and Sediri's grackle flapped his wings in protest at the other end of the shop.

Lohrna held her hand up as she downed her coffee in a few gulps, unaffected by the heat. "Listen, we can all figure this out together but it has to be *together*," she said at last, her eyes shifted from Sediri to Beejee, then finally to where Cali sat, though her gaze was a little higher than Cali's eyes. "Right?"

Cali nodded. "She's right," she said brightly. "With your wand back intact, there's nothing we can't do."

Except find the spell for you to talk to everyone, Sella thought bitterly.

Lohrna, as if reading her mind, put a gentle hand on Sella's. "It's going to be alright," she said, this time more quietly.

A shout outside broke them apart.

A prickle along Sella's scalp raced down to her feet and she felt suddenly itchy all over. She looked at Sediri, then to Lohrna and Cali who all wore expressions of worry.

Beejee was already scratching at the door.

Sella jumped off her stool and threw open the door to a chaotic scene on the once quiet street.

Poem, his hands firmly in his pockets, stared confidently at the soldiers who stood close by him. Amiri held one finger up, pointed at him like a weapon, while the others looked ready to back her up if it came down to a fight.

"I won't be going anywhere with you," Amiri said boldly. Her hand lowered though her body was still squared at him.

"And she doesn't have to," said Tate firmly. "If you think that her wyvern had anything to do with it, it is a matter for the command."

Poem's brows rose slightly. "Who do you think hired me?" he asked, his voice even and calm. "I checked your alibi. No one in your patrol can tell me *for certain* you were at the base all night. In fact, you went for a training flight for which no one can verify your whereabouts."

Amiri scoffed. "You think I flew here in the night, unseen, burned a general to death, and flew back?"

Cali gasped at Sella's side. She looked up at her. "She wouldn't!"

Sella felt an odd sense of sick voyeurism and shame. It was as though none of them, not the soldiers or the detective, noticed the people who had come out of their shops to observe the scene. Or, none of them cared. And with the ghost at her side, watching her own sister be accused of something so horrible, Sella wanted to scream until everyone else stopped yelling.

She kept the wand in her pocket, afraid of what might happen, as her fingers started to warm. She straightened her back and forced her chin higher. She took a few steps closer, making her presence known as if they were bears. "What is going on here?" she asked, as confidently as she could.

Poem's stare shifted to her. "It's none of your concern, kitchen witch."

At her feet, Beejee's tail flicked. "Detective," he corrected, loudly.

The group turned to him slowly.

Amiri's brow rose and the men behind her pulled back slightly. Still, their surprise didn't last long.

"She has a right to know the extent of your false accusations," Tate said sternly. "They all do. What you are insinuating carries a death sentence."

Wind around them blew suddenly in a blast, kicking up dust and dirt into a spiraling, stinging gust. The door to the potion shop slammed shut as Cali's hair whipped around her frame. "I won't allow this," she said, her voice so bold, Sella was sure the others could hear it too.

The group looked around them with curiosity, and… a little fear.

Lohrna moved to stand beside Sella. She looked around for Cali, her brows furrowed with worry. "It's alright," she whispered, so low Sella almost missed it as the wind died down.

Sella pulled her wand from her pocket, but she kept it hidden in the folds of her long skirt. "Poem," she said, speaking before her brain could even process her anxiety, "this is not enough to convict someone of a crime and it is irresponsible to call it out in this manner."

Poem looked at the door, then to Sella. If he understood what was happening, he kept it to himself. He looked at her as though she was the ghost. Through her. As if she didn't matter at all. "I wanted to do this quietly," he said slowly. "Her refusal to come with me speaks to her guilt."

Amiri nearly lunged at him, but Motet grabbed her hand quickly.

"Wait for us to speak to the victim, at least," Lohrna said. She stood now beside Sella with a wide stance. "That's the duty of a detective. To follow every lead and exhaust all options."

Poem's eyes narrowed. He looked at Sella now, this time, truly at her.

It sent a chill up her back.

"Can you bind the soldiers here?" he asked.

Sella jaw clenched. A binding spell? She had never used one on a living thing…

Poem waited.

"Yes," Sella said. She wasn't sure if it was a lie. But it certainly wasn't the whole truth.

TWENTY-SEVEN

The Gold Chains

"WHAT IN ALL the layers of earth was that?" Amiri leaned across the table and thrust an accusatory finger at Sella.

"Stay still," Sella grumbled as she pushed the other woman's arm away gently. With her other hand, she held her wand steady, directing it at the three soldiers. "This is not as easy as it looks."

In fact, Sella wasn't even sure it would work at all.

The military, Sella, Sediri, Lohrna and Cali in the corner, all cramped into the potion shop and away from prying eyes of the citizens who were now, Sella was certain, all gossiping about what had just occurred.

She was far from home, in a strange land of humans and wyverns and three-eyed creatures, but small towns were small towns. Here, people just seemed less open about their outrageous slander than back home. Or, perhaps, Sella thought, she just wasn't as privy to the gossip.

She closed her eyes and imagined a thin chain, gold

and glittering wrap itself around each of their wrists. She followed the chain back up to her own body, and felt a pinch as it tethered itself to her own arm. She whispered words from deep within her memory and each of them flinched.

Tate held his wrist and let out a loud shout.

Amiri side eyed him with a frown. "It doesn't hurt that badly, don't be a child."

Tate glared at her but his expression was playful nonetheless.

Motet rubbed his wrist slowly. "Did it work?"

Sella nodded. "I bound you to me," she said.

The threads that bound them to each other would hold. For now. They wouldn't be able to leave town. At least, not without dragging Sella along. The thought made her shudder.

She was only *mostly* sure that they hadn't killed Baz. And the thought of them just throwing her into a sack and flying away had to have at least crossed their minds. They didn't really know how much magic she had. It was entirely possible they might try it before it all really went bad.

Amiri looked at her hands, then to Sella's as if she was considering exactly that. But instead of grabbing her, the general simply sat up straighter in her seat. "I saw you use fire," she said. "I saw you craft it out of nothing."

"You think Sella killed Baz?" Sediri spat, uncharacteristically defensive. She leaned on the counter, crossing her arms over her chest. "With what motive or is it your prejudice getting in the way?"

Amiri's gaze was cold. "I didn't say I was making an accusation. Merely an observation. And then the wind just then? You're more powerful than you led on."

Cali stepped forward. She slipped a hand into Sella's. "Tell her," she said. "Tell her it was me and I won't let her get taken."

Sella's stomach fell. She looked down at Cali's face, hard and calm. She was certain. That much was clear. Sella took in a deep inhale until her lungs hurt. "That wasn't me," she breathed out. "The wind back there... It wasn't me."

Amiri's intense stare moved to Sediri.

"It was your sister," Sella said, this time boldly. She squeezed Cali's hand. "Your sister. Calisyali."

Amiri leaned back in her chair. Her jaw clenched. "My sister... is the Marran ghost?"

Cali smiled. "Ah! She knows me! That should make this easier!"

Sella nearly laughed with relief. With the the casual way she said it. But her blood was ice in her veins. She wondered if the others could feel it, feel the cold rush up the invisible gold links and into their hearts. "You know?"

Amiri flinched again. She swallowed hard and her words came out in bursts. "The town talks of a ghost who came with you. The witches can see her. A ghost from Marra."

"Did she know I was gone?" Cali asked. Her hand left Sella's and she made her way carefully to look across the table at her sister. She was close to her, studying her expressions. Then, she reached out and pinched Amiri's nose.

Amiri twitched. She rubbed her face with both hands. "Calisyali is gone…"

"I'm right here, actually," Cali said. "And I wish I could talk to you so I could tell you what a horrible person you've been since your arrival here. Really."

"Why don't we go upstairs?" Lohrna suggested. "Sella can make us all a cuppa and we'll get out a sheet for Cali."

"A sheet?" Amiri asked, her voice a higher pitch than Sella had heard before. Lohrna, it seemed, had managed to snap Amiri out of her spiral.

"It's hard to explain," Beejee said, sending another shock through the group. He let out a little huff, then with his tail held high, he trotted toward the stairs. "You'll just have to see it for yourself."

Lohrna smiled and followed after him.

"You don't live here anymore," Sediri called. She gave Sella a quick glare.

Amiri bit her bottom lip. Her eyes darted around the floor. "Go check on the wyverns," she said to Motet and Tate. Her stare was still far away as she took in a shaking breath.

Sella wrapped an arm around herself. It was the most vulnerable she had seen Cali's sister. It felt wrong.

"Especially Lucanairi," Amiri went on quickly. She sat up straighter, her resolve back. "We can't have any more slip ups with this detective. Go. Now."

The sound of the chairs scraping against the wood

floor snapped Sella back as Motet and Tate rose quickly and wordlessly left the shop.

"Watch this," Cali said. She knocked a chair over on her way past Sella.

Amiri flinched, and Sella held a hand over her mouth to cover to laugh.

THE PLAIN SHEET was secured over Cali's head, and, at her insistence, a pair of glasses were carefully balanced over her nose. She sat across from her sister, perfectly still while Amiri stared at her with an impossible to read expression.

Where Cali's default was to smile when hiding her true emotions, it seemed that Amiri was the opposite. She was stoic and still.

Sella and Sediri watched them and Lohrna from their place in the kitchen. The single room made it impossible to have privacy but Sella knew that Cali wanted her to stay. The two witches brewed separate pots of tea in silence, each busy infusing magic they thought would work best in a silent competition that neither acknowledged.

When they were finished, they placed their large pots of tea on the table along with several mugs for everyone to choose from.

Only Lohrna reached for one. But, she poured cups for everyone, her eyes finally moving to Amiri as she slid a mug her way. "I imagine this is a lot to take in," she said, her voice just a little too loud. "How long has it been since you've seen each other?"

Amiri blinked rapidly, her shoulders caved in as if she had just been shaken from a dream. She clutched the mug in front of her, staring into the steam as the silence took root in the spaces between them.

At last, Cali leaned in a bit. She inhaled the steam deeply.

Amiri's mouth twitched at the movement.

Sella sat beside Cali. She looked between the two sisters. "I will translate," she said. "If that's alright."

"How do I know you'll do it accurately?" Amiri raised a brow at her.

A breeze blew Amiri's hair from her shoulder. She shivered.

"Because I can also hear her," Beejee said.

"Same," Sediri said with a shrug. "You'll just have to trust that we won't lie about this."

"Get paper," the general said. "If we write the same things she says, and the cat can tell me it as well, then I'll know."

Sella sighed. It made sense that Amiri was suspicious, even more sense that she distrusted Sella particularly after what she had seen. But it didn't make her feel any less frustrated. She wanted Cali to have an easy time with all this, or at least as easy as it could be.

She looked at Sediri, who was already rummaging in her desk drawer with a grumpy expression.

With Beejee sitting at the table, and Sella and Sediri on opposite sides, and Lohrna, blindfolded, which Sella thought was a bit excessive, Amiri's body finally relaxed a little. She leaned forward, staring at Beejee rather than Cali.

"Keep your eyes on me, cat," Amiri commanded.

Beejee bristled, bared one tip of his sharp tooth but stayed quiet.

"What is our fifth brother's name?" Amiri asked.

Sella and Sediri both wrote on their papers. They folded them up and handed it to Amiri.

"We only have three brothers," Beejee said, his eyes never leaving Amiri's.

One corner of Amiri's mouth twitched up. "What were you afraid of as a child?"

Cali pulled back. She reached a hand out to the mug before her and pulled it closer slowly inching its way across the table. "I was afraid of the dark," she said.

"What else?" Amiri asked.

Cali sighed. "Being left behind. Once you all left me alone at home to go to the market because I had broken a plate."

Amiri let out a breath. Her shoulders curved inward. "Fine," Amiri said at last. She straightened back up as though the little lapse was nothing more than a momentary failure. She looked at Sella and then waved Beejee away.

Beejee tossed his head to one side, then scampered off to Lohrna. He pulled the cloth from her eyes gingerly with his teeth and then sat beside her, watching.

"I can't believe you made me admit to a deep fear in front of everyone like that," Cali said.

Sella tapped her mug lightly.

"Say it," Cali said.

Sella nodded, and did.

Amiri waved her hand. "I had to know it was you," she said. "Anyone can learn enough about names and places if they do simple reconnaissance."

"Still," Cali said bitterly.

When Sella said it, it didn't come with quite the same punch. She did her best to focus and try to be better about capturing tone. But it was easier when Cali said, "I won't let the detective take you. Or the witches. I *know* you didn't do this. You'll just have to trust me this time."

And with that, the sheet around Cali fluttered to the floor. "I'm going to go haunt this man until he leaves," her voice sounded in the room.

Sella repeated it quickly but was already standing up. "Cali, don't!"

But she was gone.

"Haunt?" Sediri said. "What does that mean, exactly, with a ghost like her?"

Sella rubbed the bridge of her nose carefully, eyes shut tight. "Last time she haunted me," she said, "I didn't sleep for two days."

"Mostly slamming cabinets and removing clothes from drawers," Beejee elaborated as he and Lohrna approached the table.

Sella lowered her hand and breathed in deeply. "Are you alright?" she asked Amiri.

Amiri's expression was stone. She rose from her seat, her hands in loose fists. "I'm fine," she said. Her voice sounded strained, as though she was trying really hard to keep herself from yelling the words. "I'm going to go make sure I don't end up as the next ghost. Thank you for the session, it was very revealing."

Lohrna moved to touch her arm but Amiri pulled away harshly.

"This bond will keep me here for now," she said, looking down at her wrist. "But I will break it if I must. I didn't kill anyone and I won't let my reputation be tarnished." She nodded to Sella and then left the group alone in the little room above the potion shop with every mug of tea still full.

TWENTY-EIGHT

The Haunting of Poem

CALI HAD BEEN HAUNTING Poem for most of the early afternoon. But their time was limited. The full moon was approaching and he didn't take the suppressant potions which meant that in a short time, he would be able to see her and, quite possibly, terrorize her back.

She shimmered into view as Sella worked to make the ingredients for the summoning spell again in the empty potion shop. "How are you?" she asked, her gaze drifting to Cali for a moment before she refocused on crushing spice in her gray bowl.

"Well, I was surprised by the difficulty with which it was to move any of his items. Is there a warding spell or something around him?" Cali hopped onto the counter and watched Sella work.

Sella shook her head. "I meant… How are you? After talking to your sister?"

Cali shrugged. "I'm fine," she said.

The witch's hands continued to work at the ingredients, focusing on getting each proportion correct. She wanted to say that Cali and her sister were so similar for being so different. Both had a strange ability to compartmentalize things. Cali masked hers with a smile, and Amiri seemed to simply push it away, stuff it down until it couldn't resurface.

"Where's Lohrna?" Cali changed the subject.

"Off to get you," Sella said softly.

"Oops."

"And bring Poem for this spell. We need to get Baz back as soon as possible after…"

"Everything," Cali finished for her.

Sella nodded. "Yes, after everything."

SELLA HELD her wand in her hand, pointed loosely at the ghost of Baz.

He looked as he did in life, if not slightly translucent, the hint of a shimmer twinkling from around his outline.

Sella was grateful. She had worried that he would appear before them burnt and angry. But instead, he seemed serene, his skin the same as it was when he was alive. Almost. She wanted to ask him what it was like on the other side. If he was happy, if it was scary. If those she loved were there. If Cali would be happier there, too.

But instead, she looked at the group around her with wide eyes but everyone was too busy gawking at the ghost before them to pay her any attention. Apparently, even the non-witches could see him.

It worked. And now, if the spell had been done right, there were only three questions to ask.

Poem nodded to Sella.

She took a deep breath, her fingers tightened around the wand. "Do you know who killed you?"

Baz's eyes focused. He looked at her with a faint smile. "Yes."

Sella's wand lowered. Her heart began to beat faster. "Do you know why?"

Baz's gaze moved to the others in the room, looking at each with a thoughtful stare before turning again to Sella. "No."

Sella paused. It would be too easy if he had, wouldn't it? But he did know his killer. Someone close to him, then, or someone he had interacted with before. Still, he didn't know the motive. So… it couldn't have been someone he had wronged. Right?

Poem stepped forward. "Do you know what you'll ask next?" he whispered.

"No," Baz said. And like smoke, he disappeared into the air.

The room was silent.

Slowly, each head turned to Poem.

Beejee was the first to speak. "Are you stupid?"

Poem closed his eyes. His head lowered.

"In case you didn't notice," Beejee said, "that was a question."

Poem sighed.

Lohrna pinched her brow. She shook her head. "Can we do it again?" she asked, her voice hopeful.

Sella deflated.

"No," Beejee said. "We cannot."

Lazil scratched the back of her bald head. "Well, so there's that. Now we know that it's not just the summoner that can ask the question. An honest mistake."

Verol picked up her familiar and held her close. "I didn't think we needed to be *that* clear," she said slowly. "Once the spell is cast, it's done. Baz's spirit requires rest. All dead things do. We cannot summon him again. Not for a very, very long time."

"How long?" Lazil asked.

"A very long time," Verol grumbled. "What are we going to do now? We have no witness, no leads, no mot—"

Sella's eyes narrowed slightly. She was going to say 'no motive' but had stopped herself. And she understood why. Verol had plenty of motive, a whole barn's worth.

TWENTY-NINE

Full Moon Clue Hunt

Sella laid on her bed with one arm draped over her head. After all of that work, they were no closer to solving this. Except, maybe, Amiri seemed like slightly less of an obvious suspect. Maybe.

Lohrna stretched out on her own bed, her legs were up against the wall, tapping the clay lightly with her heels. "Poem isn't exactly the brightest star is he?"

Sella let out a heavy breath, letting out all the air in her lungs until she felt her body sink lower into the bed.

"He knew who the killer was, but he didn't know why they killed him…" Lohrna repeated the clues. "That was kind of useless. I'm sorry you had to expel so much energy for that."

Sella turned to her friend, her arm still covered her eyes. "I'm less tired than usual," she said. "It must be the wand."

"Well, that's something to be thankful for," Lohnra said.

Beejee jumped on the foot of the bed. His weight pressed down near Sella's legs. "The reason for his death could still be obvious even if he didn't know it. Maybe Baz was as foolish as Poem and missed something clear."

"Who in town did he know?" Lohrna asked. "Amiri and the other soldiers. Verol… maybe some other villagers if he'd had run-ins with them in the past?"

Sella opened one eye. "If he didn't know why he was killed, I think it's fair to rule out the military. For now. I would think *that* would be easy for him to figure out. Tate or Motet for their last fight they had with him. Amiri for power."

"And Verol for the barn burning," Lohnra added.

"True," Beejee said. "What about Cosas? He started the recent fire. Perhaps it got out of hand before too?"

"In a building like that?" Lohrna asked. "Where only he burned?"

Beejee's ear twitched.

Lohrna rolled to her stomach, propping herself up on her elbows. "I'll clue hunt tonight," she said.

"But… It's a full moon tonight."

"Cali says they're more accepting here," Lohrna said. "Becides, I think I could put my nose to use."

"I'll go with you," Beejee said, a protective tone in his voice. "I can use magic if anyone tries to harm you."

"And I'll use my teeth," Lohrna said with a laugh. She gnashed her jaws dramatically.

Sella smiled, though the heaviness remained in her limbs. "Do you think Poem will be doing the same?"

"Maybe," Lohrna said. "I wonder if he's a mouse…"

Sella remembered their time in Marra, where a leader of a society of shifters had used his mouse form for nefarious purposes. Most egregiously, he oversalted everyone's soup on the day of the big contest and they had to host a redo. Her smile grew. "I hope so," she said at last. "Then he'd be able to find something we missed low to the ground."

Lohrna sighed. "What if it was just spontaneous combustion? Like all of his anger and bad nature finally exploded out of him?"

Beejee glared at her.

Lohrna sat up at last with a loud groan. "What, it could happen?"

The last of the light from the small window began to fade from yellow to pink as the sun set in the distance. Lohrna and Beejee both turned to the beam of light.

"We better get going," Beejee said. "Otherwise, I don't think you'll fit through the door."

Lohrna let out a small chuckle. She smoothed out her dress. "Oh, you're right," she said. She looked around the room. "Cal, do you want to come too? It might be good for you to get your mind working."

"She's not here," Beejee said. He ushered Lohrna toward the door. "She'll find us if she wants to."

Lohrna nodded. "Well, how about we meet in the field outside of town when the moon is half way in the sky?" she said. "It'll give you time to rest but time to talk, too."

Sella nodded and closed her eyes. "Good plan," she

said and then she heard the door close slowly behind her familiar and her friend.

SELLA AWOKE WITH A JUMP. She hadn't even realized that she had fallen asleep until she was awake, the sky outside dark, and the room a little cold. She waved her hand and little fires burst to life around the room, quickly warming the air and lighting the space in a glow.

Cali appeared beside her, staring up at the ceiling. "I'm not afraid of the dark anymore," she whispered.

Sella's head rolled to her. "No?"

Cali's eyes moved to Sella. "No," she said. "But sometimes I am still afraid of being left behind."

Sella looked back up at the plain tan ceiling. "Me too," she said honestly.

It was strange, she thought, for them to both be afraid of being forgotten when they were the ones who had left. She wasn't sure what it meant, or if it meant nothing. But for now, she moved her hand to rest on Cali's.

The ghost nuzzled closer until her nose rested in the crook of Sella's neck, sending a fire through her body.

"When you're ready," Sella said, "Lohrna said to meet her in the field."

Cali nodded and snuggled in. "In a moment," she whispered.

THIRTY

No Talk of Murder Tonight

CLOUDS COVERED the sky but it was still bright enough with the powerful full moon shimmering through to see the open field in shades of gray. In the open air outside the town, a massive wolf-like Lohrna loomed over Sella, Cali, and Beejee. She was several heads taller than Sella when standing on her four slender legs, a thick coat of silver and dark gray fur covered her body, and her long tail wagged gently in the night air.

It has become their monthly ritual to spend the whole evening together on the nights that Lohrna shifted. Sella was sure that, though they wanted to help, Cali and Lohrna were both frustrated with half of the night being used to look around for clues.

This was their only opportunity to speak to one another, thanks to the strange spell that allowed familiars to speak and the fact that most animals could see Cali's form.

"Did your nose find anything useful?" Cali asked, her

tone filled with joy, despite the sinister topic of conversation.

Lohrna shook her head, her snout nearly hitting Sella's shoulder. "No," she said, her voice deep. "But, that is the strange part. I went to the scene of the crime. I didn't smell anything out of the ordinary. So, if someone used an accelerant for the fire, the smell of it was long gone."

"Thank the rain," Cali said with a smile. "I really didn't want to talk about clues or murder tonight."

Lohrna smiled back, exposing a row of sharp dog teeth. It would be terrifying, if Lohrna didn't happen to also look, at least a little, like her usual goofy self.

Sella sat down on the warm sand and Beejee curled up in her lap, both content to simply be.

"Same," Lohrna said. "I was hoping to talk to you about your sister. How are you feeling about everything? Nervous? Excited? Want me to go give her a scare for you?"

Cali laughed. She looked up at the sky and shook her head. "No, but thank you." She sighed and leaned up against Lohrna, nuzzling into her fur. "Honestly?"

Lohrna nodded.

Cali sighed. "Honestly, I feel like… everything. And nothing all at once."

Beejee's gaze drifted up to Sella.

Cali went on, "I want to tell her how I don't care that she doesn't care that I'm gone. But that shows I care, doesn't it?"

"It's alright to care," Lohrna said softly, a low growl

deep in her throat. "And it's alright to care that it looks like you don't, too."

Cali wrapped an arm around Lohrna's head. "I suppose," she said. "The good thing about being the only one in a situation like this is that no one gets to tell me what is right or wrong."

A long silence filled the darkness around them. Overhead, clouds parted and the empty land was lit by silver moonlight. Sella looked around, waiting for something. A wyvern, perhaps… or a mob ready to come after them.

She hadn't felt safe since the discovery of Baz. It was as though she was just waiting for the next terrible thing to happen.

Beejee pawed at her arm. "Pretend you're among the music," he whispered. "Calm down."

Sella breathed in deeply. He was right. Here, and now, in the moonlight with her family, she was safe. She let it out in a sigh that no one but Beejee seemed to notice. A wave of peace flowed over her. She felt the corners of her lips turn up. It had gotten easier over the years to find her calm.

"I left them all long ago," Cali said at last. "But if I hadn't, they would have left me. There was no room for things like compassion or family ties there. Unless those ties could get you a higher rank in the military. I was fine not seeing any of them again."

"And now that you have…" Lohrna prompted.

Cali exhaled. "I'm grieving it all over again, I think."

"It makes sense to me," Lohrna said. "Perhaps Sella has a blend for that."

Cali and Lohrna both turned to her.

"For grief?" Sella said. "I think that just has to be felt."

"How about we keep working on the signature blend," Cali said. "The lucky brew. And… maybe we'll get lucky?"

Sella laughed. "That'll be the day."

"But you did promise Sediri," Cali said. "And that will be one more good deed in our favor."

"Maybe we find a spell to turn your sister into a toad," Beejee finally spoke up. "Just for a little while."

Cali giggled. "Is there one for that?"

Sella scratched behind Beejee's ear. Though his tail thumped against her leg, his cheek leaned into her hand. "No, but it's a fun idea."

"Too bad," Cali said wistfully.

Lohrna lay on the ground beside Sella. She curled into a crescent and huffed, a puff of dust blew around her like a halo in the silver glow.

Cali rested on her thick shoulder, easing into the fur.

"Any progress on the luck spell?" Lohrna asked after Cali had been still a while.

"Maybe I'll get lucky and luck my way into the perfect blend?"

Lohrna snorted, another small cloud of dirt breezed around her. "I'm still dreaming of those snacks from the market… When do you think it'll open again?"

Sella smiled. "Hopefully soon. We don't have anything like that back home, huh?"

"We do not," Lohrna said. "But maybe you can snag

some recipes before we go. Start serving those up at your shop."

Beejee perked up. "Finally. *There's* a good idea."

THIRTY-ONE

Sella Has Too Many Nicknames

"Are you worried?" Sella asked Amiri.

The two were at the counter of the potion shop, awaiting Sediri's coffee as the witch worked to prepare their brew.

The small space was filled with the rich smell of spice and cinnamon. Sediri had put too much confidence in. Sella could feel it in the air, smell it on the steam.

Amiri leaned on the counter with her hip. She crossed her arms over her chest and eyed Sella with her usual hint of suspicion. "Well, your sister being dead certainly puts things into perspective," she said.

Sella looked away. She didn't have any siblings, but she could only imagine the heartbreak of losing Lohrna, the closest thing she had to a sister. It must be immense. Too much to hold.

Perhaps Sediri had been correct to add the extra dose of confidence to the blend.

"But… if you're convicted..?" Sediri's eyes shifted from Sella to Amiri.

Amiri sighed, it sounded so strange compared to her usual powerful persona. She pushed off the counter and her wide stance was back as Sediri slid a mug toward her. "Then we need to find the real killer," she said casually.

Sella took her own cup of coffee and sipped it quickly. She needed the extra self-assurance.

Sediri pulled her long hair into a low bun at the base of her neck. She looked at them with her eyes shining. "He knew his killer, he doesn't know why, he was killed with fire," she repeated. "Well, that rules you out at least, doesn't it, fire starter? You didn't know him."

"Your nicknames are getting old," Sella said.

Amiri held her coffee closer. "You do seem like a likely culprit," she said. "You use fire, and the witches here have had run-ins with Baz in the past. Who's to say you weren't hired to come here to kill him?"

"Well, me, for one," Cali said, appearing beside them in a flash.

Amiri shivered.

Sediri was quick to point at the ghost. "Your sister is here."

Amiri turned to the space where Cali stood, though it was clear she was looking through her.

"And I'm not sure you're aware," Sediri went on. "But you're kind of getting on her bad side here."

Cali crossed her arms. "I wouldn't quite say that—"

Amiri crossed hers as well, accidentally mirroring her younger sister.

"What do the others think?" Sella asked, in part to change the subject, in part to get more information in a way she hoped seemed seamless.

"That you seem suspect," Amiri said without hesitation.

"No!" Cali cried. A wind burst through the shop, knocking over a few trinkets along the shelves.

Amiri flinched, she wrapped one arm around herself and looked at the knocked over items with her brows knit.

"Sella came here to help," Cali's voice was steady now, though her hair and clothes still blew around her in a frenzy. "She came here to help."

Sella hurried to Cali's side. She held the ghost close. "I'm fine," she whispered.

Amiri looked from Sella to the space where Cali's head would be, then back. "I didn't mean…" she paused, her hand falling to her side.

Sediri leaned forward, her smile almost eager. "They have a right to be suspicious of us," she said. "I heard there's tension. But we're not letting anyone come for Sella."

"I didn't say I would," Amiri said. "Only, look at the evidence."

"We're. Not. Letting. Them." Sediri tapped the counter with each word.

Amiri pulled back, then nodded as her eyes found Sella again. "Right," she said quietly. "We're not letting them." She fished a few coins from her pocket and tossed them on the counter. "I'll see what I can find," she said and left the shop without casting a second glance at Sella.

Sediri stood taller as soon as the door shut behind Amiri. "Alright with that out of the way," she said, her smiling growing, "Sella, pick up those things that Cali blew over. And, tides. Would you two stop clinging to each other? It was barely an accusation from an already accused woman."

Cali sniffled. She side eyed Sella who gave her one small squeeze, then let go. Cali laughed. "I did overreact there, didn't I?"

Sella smiled and moved to pick up the few little items that had fallen.

"Sella," Sediri said as she poured herself another cup of coffee. "I was thinking about this spell that we use to bring people back for questions three." She sprinkled a little sugar in her cup and swirled it with her hand hovering above the liquid. "Would you be able to recreate it for me?"

Sella looked up from her crouched position, a small statue of a wolf still in her hand.

"Not to use right away," Sediri explained. "When I'm ready to do it myself, I'll cast it. But, I'd like to gather all the ingredients and prepare it before you leave. You were always better about the precise things."

Sella went back to tidying. "I could do that for you, but you would need to add the roots that Verol gave us at the end on your own. I think the recipe called for it to be fresh," she said.

"I can do that much," Sediri said confidently. "I swear, you think so little of me after all I've done for you." She sounded a lot like the old women in her town, scolding her for not being grateful enough as a child for whatever strange thing she never understood.

Sella put the little wolf back on the shelf next to a large shimmering lavender crystal. "May I ask why?"

"You may," Sediri said. "But I won't answer."

Sella snorted. That sounded about right.

MAKING the spell for the third time turned out to be surprisingly easy. She was glad to be able to make it in the comfort of their hotel room, away from the other witches, the military, and detective.

Sella made a mental note to pack up the ingredients that she didn't have in Marra to bring home just in case their detective skills were ever needed again. A simple 'yes' or 'no' wasn't exactly going to make things easy, but it was better than nothing. She only wondered how diffi-cult it would be to find the few ingredients that needed to be fresh. How fresh was 'fresh' afterall?

But, as she packed up the spells for Sediri, she found herself drawn back to the table. It was easy enough, ulti-mately. And she had all the necessary ingredients now with no guarantee of getting them again. She could make one more... though part of her wasn't even sure why she wanted to.

Like Cali, she had left her home and only come back after it was too late. Her mother was gone already, the shop was closed, and her childhood home was guarded by a magic so powerful, she took one look at it upon her return and left it there to rot for a year. She had been gone so long that even when she returned, a part of her thought they'd leave again. And this time for good.

But she knew now she'd stay. Stay in the little port town by the sea with its strange and loving inhabitants, its pixie problem and portals to libraries, and siren statues that, more often than not, she thought about smashing. It was home, but it would never be the same. She had changed and it had changed.

"What're you thinking about?" Cali asked.

Sella looked over the spell. It was silly to be thinking about this now with so many other things happening but she couldn't take the thought once it entered her mind. Three questions. What would she ask?

THIRTY-TWO

The Three Questions

SELLA PREPARED the spell with relative ease, though her back started to ache and her eyes were strained. She stood beside Cali and Lohrna now, with Beejee firmly at her feet, confident in a way she would never know. She wasn't confident at all. If anything, she was beginning to think she was making a terrible mistake.

"Are you ready for this?" Cali asked as if reading her thoughts. She put a hand around Sella's waist, resting her head gently on her shoulder.

The small gesture filled Sella with warmth, despite the chill of Cali's closeness. She took in a long breath. "I don't know what to ask," she said at last. She held the wand tighter as Cali's hand traced her back.

The ghost moved to look up at her. "I think that's fair," Cali said. "Why don't you wait and see what comes to you when you see her?"

Lohrna placed a hand on Sella's shoulder. "We'll be

here through it and when it's done," she said. "If you want to do this, you have us with you."

Sella's jaw tightened. "It's now or never," she said through gritted teeth.

Cali nodded. "I'll be right here," she said. "I'll stay with you."

Sella read the spell aloud, and in a swirling mist, Sella's mother appeared before them.

She looked the same as she appeared in Sella's fondest memories of her. She was youthful looking, healthy, free of burns across her face. But the more Sella looked, the more her mother looked like… a ghost. She was somewhat unclear, her image rippling slowly as if she was underwater staring at her through the gentle waves of the ocean. She looked at Sella, then to Cali, then Lohrna, but with what expression, Sella couldn't tell.

Perhaps she was upset at being awoken from wherever she came from. Or was happy to see Sella. Or confused. Perhaps she felt nothing at all and this before her wasn't really her mother but merely an echo.

Her eyes moved to the wand in Sella's hand.

No, Sella thought. This was her mother after all.

She held the hand out with an open palm. "Are you surprised to see this in my hand?"

"No," her mother said.

Sella looked down at the wand, at the fine details of the wood, the glittering place where it had been broken. Her mother had given it to another witch before she had died. She didn't leave it for Sella and no matter how badly Sella wanted to ask why, that was simply an answer she would never have. Like so many other questions that swirled within her, all would go unanswered and unresolved.

Her brows furrowed as she combed through her mind in search of another question. She looked up at her mother's face, moving across the shifting details and catching a few things that stayed steady. Her impassive eyes. Her scarless face. "Were you afraid of me?" Sella's voice shook as she asked it. She wasn't even sure she knew where that question came from. All she knew was that she needed an answer.

"No," the ghost said. A little grin crept onto her lips, so subtle, Sella almost missed it.

The grip on Sella's shoulder tightened as Lohrna gave her a quick smile as though she knew what the answer would have been to that question all along.

And perhaps she did. Lohrna had never been afraid either.

"Can I..." Sella paused. She didn't know, couldn't specify what she was asking for. Could she solve this case? Could she find the spell for Cali? Could she bring the witches and the military, even this small squad, together? Could she make it home safe? "Can I do this?" Sella breathed.

Her mother extended a hand toward the group. She smiled brightly and began to disappear like a slow, steady stream leaving a teacup. "Yes," her voice said.

The group was silent for a long moment as Sella sank slowly onto the bed. She held her head in her hands and simply breathed as Beejee curled up beside her.

Lohrna gave her shoulder another little squeeze. "Want to talk about it?"

Sella shook her head. "Not really," she said at last. She lifted her chin up and pushed away the beginnings of tears from her eyes. "I feel… foolish."

"Why?" Both Cali and Lohrna asked at once.

Sella let out a heavy breath. She stared down at her wand. "I don't know. I rush into things. Like this. I should have thought longer about what to ask."

Lorhna sat down next to her. Her hand wrapped around Sella's shoulders and she pulled her into her arms like she had seen Aadel do to her many times as a child.

Sella felt small and angry and at peace all at once.

Cali kneeled in front of her and held Sella's knees with cold hands. "No one ever gets the closure they want," she said softly. "But you heard her. You can do this. Whatever you set your mind to. It'll be alright even if you don't have any of the answers you want."

Beejee pressed his forehead into Sella's chest. He purred gently and Sella let a tear escape her eye.

"We should get the spell to Sediri," she said at last.

She could do this.

She'd have to.

THIRTY-THREE

Always

Black Feather Potions & Pastries was still open when the group arrived, spell in hand.

At the bar, Poem sat, still as a statue. He was gazing into his cup and Sediri, her familiar perched upon her shoulder, seemed to be largely ignoring him as she tended her mortar and pestle, crushing up some herb that smelled faintly of mint and citrus.

Lohrna took her seat beside him and with a smile clearly meant to bring Sella out of her dark mood, she loudly asked, "What are you drinking?"

"Poison, for all I know," he answered dryly.

Lohrna pulled back as though she had been smacked. "What?"

Sella slid the potion to Sediri silently and she took it without a second glance, storing it away under her counter in one fluid motion. Sediri went back to crushing up the bright purple flowering herb.

"Why would I poison you in my own shop?" she said

with a sardonic quirk of her brow. "Wouldn't it be better to do it in the tavern where everyone has access to your cup?"

"Yes," Poem said quietly. "Poison… Who would ever suspect the cook?" Poem went on quietly, almost as though simply musing to himself. "But Baz wasn't poisoned, it's the perfect ruse."

Sella's brows furrowed. "Which cook are you speaking of?"

"The only one who uses fire like that," Poem said.

"The old man Cosas? What?" Lohrna asked in disbelief.

Poem's eyes were fixed on the door. "I should have seen it this whole time. I'm a fool to not see it before."

"You're a fool alright, but not for the reasons you think," Beejee said as he jumped up onto the table. His tail flicked. "Are you just going to keep pointing your finger at everyone?"

"Think about it," Poem said, as though he hadn't heard the familiar at all. "Baz knew him, he had been to this town before. But didn't know the motive. It makes perfect sense."

"In what way?" Lohrna asked. Her tone was harsher than usual. "Because of the fire? Is that all? What possible motive could he have? He's an old man. And nice."

Poem's gaze drifted lazily to her. "I haven't figured out that part yet," he said. "Retribuitin of some kind, I'm sure. Are he and Verol close?"

Lohrna shook her head. "You're reaching."

"Do you have a better suspect?" Poem said. "I don't

see you helping at all, even with this supposed detective agency you have."

Sella let out a heavy breath. "Poem, we need to think things through before we make any accusations. We know, *directly*, how damaging it can be for rumors like that to spread. Keep this to yourself until you actually have any evidence."

"What evidence? Everything at the scene was burnt," Poem said. His usual collected demeanour was gone. "All of this will be circumstantial."

"Nothing at the scene was burnt except Baz. Which, kind of rules out the oil accelerant. There's no way Cosas would be able to do this without the entire forge catching fire." Sella studied his face, the way his wrinkles at his forehead deepened, the hard line of his lips.

Cali shimmered beside Sella. "Why is he in such a rush to point accusations all over the place? Did he hear from the commanders or something? Are we under a tighter deadline than we originally thought?"

Sella cocked her head.

"Get it? *Dead*line?"

The witch let out a little snort. "Must be," she whispered.

"Listen, pressure is mounting from the command," Poem answered as if he had heard her. "I received a letter today. They need to hold a trial soon. They appear ineffective without the culprit in custody for this long."

"Right," Sella said slowly. "But we're not going to just sacrifice up someone for the sake of closure on their end."

Poem's eyes were wild. They darted back to his coffee, getting lost in the dark liquid.

Sediri added the herbs to the pot beside her. She struck a flint below it and it warmed quickly, filling the space with a cocooning effect of scent and warmth. Her hands wrapped around the pot and she closed her eyes, breathing so deeply her chest rose and fell roughly.

"Someone did this," Poem said. "Someone did this…"

Sediri opened her eyes at once and immediately shot a glare at the detective before she stood taller and plastered a smile to her face. "Here," Sediri said as she poured him a fresh cup. "Drink this."

Sella eyed the cup, then her gaze flicked back to Sediri who ignored her in turn.

The other witch's eyes were fixed on Poem. "Go on," she urged.

Poem looked at her, then to his cup. He grabbed it with shaking hands and drank it quickly despite the heat. "Oh," he whispered when he finished. "This is…" His eyes rolled back and his head hit the counter.

"Tides!" Lohrna leaped out of her seat. "He's dead!"

Sediri waved her hand dismissively. "Nonsense," she said casually. "He just had too much caffeine and was starting to get jumpy. Verol gave me this herb, it's a powerful sedative, when used properly."

Sella rubbed her temples. "You sedated *the detective?*"

Sediri scoffed. "Of course I did, you saw how he was behaving." She leaned down to get a look at him more closely. "He should be waking up in a bit. It doesn't last long."

"What will you tell him when he wakes up? That you basically poisoned him?" Sella was nearly shouting now.

Lohrna's hands were still clasped over her mouth.

"I'll tell him the truth," Sediri said. "He was out of hand and needed sleep." She faced Sella with a fire in her eyes. "You heard him, we have a limited time to figure this out before someone innocent gets hurt." She shooed the group away. "Go on, then," she said. "Solve this."

"You know," Lohrna said as they exited the shop, "Sediri might actually be insane."

Beejee trotted ahead with his tail held high. "I like it," he said.

"I'm glad you're on our side," Lohrna said, a lightness back in her tone.

Beejee turned over his shoulder. "Always."

THIRTY-FOUR

Flames Follow All the Way Home

THE TAVERN WAS BUSY. Lively conversations filled the space, though, Sella noticed with a dull ache in her chest, that they were not the voices she had grown familiar with back home. New cadences of speaking, new sounds, new names. Behind the counter, Verol was working hard, busily pouring drinks, offering refills, and gossiping with patrons. It reminded her of the way Hazen would work all night with the same cheerful smile, never letting on his fatigue as the night wore on.

But it wasn't Hazen's.

Sella missed his laugh, and stern talks. The music from the corner that some enthusiastic young person would strum on their strings and sing about love and heartache too big for the world to hold, as if they knew of anything outside the small town by the sea.

But she realized now that perhaps love and heartache knew no boundary and no small town could contain its depth. She tried to remember some of the lyrics, but she had never paid enough attention then and so the melody fled from her mind as soon as she tried to collect it.

She missed the spiderwebs on the rafters. She missed the shadows she knew and the spaces where she could hide. She missed the firelight… And all at once, in a room full of people, alongside witches who accepted her as she was, and in a land where she was needed, she felt utterly alone and useless.

She had decided to come here tonight in the hopes of hearing some moment of someone slipping up, seeing some flinch that someone would make without noticing, finding some internal feeling that could guide her to the next choice, the next thing to do. But she sat there, quiet and still, not moving either in her body or her mind.

She looked down at her hands on the table. The way they held her cup like it was a rope pulling her from the waters. She loosened her grasp and sighed out the feeling of emptiness within her heart.

It was going to be alright. Things were going to be alright. She had come to find the spell to help Cali. A death, however politically important to them, had to come second. It just had to. Because the thought of Cali feeling this type of loneliness for so long was beginning to break her.

All at once, her mind began to twist around itself.

She shouldn't have come alone.

"Sella," the detective voice startled her from her thoughts. His definitive tone sounded almost rude as though he were talking to a beast. He stood by the table, his brows slightly furrowed as if he was annoyed that she hadn't heard him approach. Perhaps he had been calling to her for a while.

She couldn't be sure.

Poem didn't notice, or care about her discomfort. He went on, casually, "Have you heard the theory that the culprit of a crime tends to try to insert themselves in the investigation?"

Her eyes narrowed in response. She squared her shoulders in her seat, not ready to stand just yet, but absolutely not willing to let him see her nervous. She was silent. She didn't like where he was going with this, though she had the sinking feeling since the death that this was where it would lead eventually.

A half smile cracked his face, as if he found the whole thing mildly amusing. But not even fun enough for a full smile and, somehow, that annoyed her even more. "No, you probably don't know such things. You're from a small town on a small island," Poem said.

Sella's hand tightened around her wand. She knew she wouldn't need it if it came down to it. But in a strange way, she felt that it held her back. There was no warmth flooding into her hand. No pounding heartbeat driving her forward. Just the feel of the smooth wood against her hand and the slight indent at where it had been broken. "What are you insinuating?" she asked at last.

She wanted to hear him say it. He had accused almost everyone, yet held back with her. It bothered her.

There was no reply. Poem stood beside her and looked out at the crowd. His eyes seemed to be searching for something he could not find, no matter how hard he looked.

Sella knew the feeling. And though he had just nearly accused her of a crime, one punishable beyond belief, Sella couldn't help but feel a kind of strange closeness with him. They both looked out at the groups of people, feeling alone, looking for something beyond their sight. By how far, though, for either of them, Sella couldn't be sure.

She had to simply hope that she was close. That if she kept going, something was going to break in the best way.

"Why did you stay?" he asked, still avoiding looking at her.

Sella stared out with him. "I wanted to help," she spoke softly.

At last, Poem's eyes moved to look at her in his periphery. "Is that so?"

Sella let out a small breath. She took a long drink of wine, feeling the burn in her throat echo out into her limbs. She set her glass down with a hard thud. "I wanted to help. I'll leave it up to you to decide who I want to help the most. You won't believe any answer I give you." She kept her hands wrapped around the cup, feeling it warm slightly under her fingers. Her words were bold but her heart beat quickly in her ribs. She looked up at him, her stare hard. "I won't let you take me down for what happened to Baz."

"No?"

Sella set her jaw. She looked back out at the people in the tavern, laughing and smiling, their faces shining in the candlelight. "And I won't let you take the wrong person down for it either." She pushed herself up from her seat, facing him directly now. As she looked at him closely, she noticed the lines in his face, the weariness in the puff around his eyes. But there was a shimmer in his eye, a cockiness that she didn't like. "Good evening, detective," she said and pushed past him.

"Good evening, fire witch."

Sella did not stop or turn back. She walked through the crowd and out the door into the night. But where she expected to be met with a chill as she would back home, it was only the warm night air, thick with distant rain, that greeted her.

Still, habit compelled her to wrap an arm around herself as she walked down the empty road toward the hotel with a sense of dread and anger worming its way into her. Now this, she thought bitterly, was the feeling she knew well.

She looked up at the sky, it was dark, impossibly so with the thick clouds hanging low. She wondered if the wyverns were up there above it all, able to see the moon and stars when no one else could. She wondered if the riders were with them and what it must be like to feel closer to the sky.

Sella sighed and her hand lowered from her body and for the quickest moment, she saw the shimmer of the gold chain around her wrist tethering her to them. She continued her walk, listening to the sound of her boots against the strange stone and feeling the unease with which her steps landed. She didn't know the grooves of the road the way she did back home.

She flicked her wrist and three little fires burst forth from her fingertips. They hovered beside her, floating in the open air like feathers. She smiled as the space around her illuminated in the warm glow. She lit these fires every morning in her shop back home, and every evening in the loft above. She had never made them out in the open. "Follow me home," she commanded with as much authority as she could muster.

She continued her walk and the fires floated alongside her.

A swell of pride rose from her stomach and up to her chin that she held higher now.

Sella, the kitchen witch with the affinity for fire. Sella, the witch who kept messing up. Sella, the witch who found herself in strange places. Sella, so unlucky and selfish.

No, perhaps tonight, she would just be Sella. No modifiers. No judgments. Just Sella.

THIRTY-FIVE

'Worthless' is a Matter of Perspective

"Did you find anything?" Beejee asked when she returned to their little hotel room.

She shook her head. "You?"

"No, the market is basically empty," he answered as his tail flicked.

Beejee and Lohrna sat on the bed together. Their mission had been to scout out the market, while Cali had intended to use her 'ghostly powers', as she had called them, to keep an eye on Tate and Motet.

Splitting up had been her idea but it hadn't paid off. She flopped onto the opposite bed and groaned into the down pillow as a little sharp feather poked through and pierced her cheek. Her fingers fumbled with it until she managed to pinch the hollow shaft and pluck it free. Sella rolled over and turned the little, fluffy black feather in between her fingers.

"But," Lohrna said, bright as ever. "It was not a total loss. I did find a crystal vendor!" She bounced up from the bed and grabbed her bag that had been resting on the table.

Sella's gaze shifted to the bag, only realizing now that it was *very* full. "Did you–"

Lohrna cut her off with a wave of her hand. "Well, Beejee says it was a waste, but I thought the vendor was quite fascinating. Cali would have loved him. I said I had a friend that used to be in the rare gem business, and his prices went down *significantly* after that."

"He was trying to swindle you," Beejee said as he hopped onto the table and watched Lohrna pulling various shiny crystals from her bag.

Lohrna shrugged. "I have to admire the business model," she said with a light laugh. "No bad feelings." She showed off a pink rock to Sella. It was a little bigger than Lohrna's hand, flecks of gold deposit caught the light as she turned it over. "This one is supposed to help with love. I better put this at the bottom of the bag. I don't want to end up like Sediri, falling in love with a human…" Her eyes flicked up to Sella. "Oh, no offense."

Cali materialized through the wall, only half her body sticking through. "None taken," she said. "I'm a *super*human."

"Cali's here," Sella said with a smile. "And she says she's a superhuman so it's fine."

Lohrna waved the ghost over. "Come look at these," she said as her smile grew even wider. She put her hands on her hips, looking proud of her collection.

Cali examined the rocks, all different shapes and

colors, some dull, some shining in the firelight. "None of these are—"

"The man said they were all pretty common here, and he brought the price down when I mentioned I had a friend in the industry," Lohnra spoke over her, her voice a little too loud. "But I think they'll look great in my collection."

Cali nodded, her eyes were soft. "They will," she said.

Lohrna turned to the space where Cali stood. "Please tell me you were snooping on the soldiers and one of them confessed that they did it, though," Lohrna said quickly.

Cali and Sella shook their heads.

"No, they're surprisingly… Wholesome?" Cali said with a little shrug. "They seem to like the small town here and are kind of upset at their bad reputation and that no one will talk to them."

When Beejee explained, Lohrna looked glum. "I didn't think about their perspective on this," she said. "They must be always going from place to place— coming here should be like a vacation. Except for you know—"

"The murder," Beejee finished for her.

"Right," Lohrna said. "Except for that." She sat back down on the bed, her eyes were still locked on her rocks at the table. "I've been thinking about it," she said softly. "Do you think that this place will be better when we leave?"

Sella rose a brow. "What do you mean?"

Lohrna sighed, her curls fell over her shoulders as her head fell slightly. "I just wonder about this place. I hope they'll be alright when we leave. Or, I hope they'll be better because we came. Not worse."

Cali sat beside her, her expression weary with concern. "I think this would have happened if we were here or not," she said. "We can't blame ourselves for things we had no control over."

"I wish we had Seaglass," Sella said with a small smile after she translated for Cali. "I never thought I'd say that, but I do. They would say something strange but helpful now."

Beejee's ear flicked. He sat up a little taller. "I can be vaguely ominous if that helps," he said.

Sella fell back on the bed, twirling the feather in her hand again. "Go for it," she said with a laugh.

THIRTY-SIX

The Loyalty of a Kitchen Witch

SELLA's back was starting to ache. She had been hunched over the ingredients for too long, trying a little of this herb, a more heavily crushed version of that one, and going back to the several open books stacked around her trying to find the right recipe, or even a hint of a recipe.

It had been consuming her most of the morning and she hadn't slept much the past few nights. The toll was beginning to show on her body and in her posture. She was glad that Lohrna had stayed in bed when she left this morning, and that Cali was still, she hoped, resting wherever she did when she wasn't with her.

Sella took another sip of her coffee, her eyes still locked on the pages. She had to get one win soon. And after her discussion with Lohrna the night before, she was determined to leave this place just a little better than she found it.

Sediri's footsteps, light and easy, came from behind her. "I'm glad to see you're still working on the signature blend you promised me," she said as she tossed a lock of hair behind her shoulder. "Afterall, you did promise."

Sella looked up. "I promised to do my best," she said. "I didn't promise to deliver if it can't be done."

Sediri's eyes narrowed slightly. She strode past Sella and to the coffee pot, breathing in deeply. "Focus?" she asked.

Sella nodded, already nose buried in her potion again. "And serenity."

"Serenity?" Sediri pulled back from the pot as though it was poison. "Whatever for?"

Sella was busy angling the tip of her knife down at the mushroom before her. She had to be careful to only get the stringy part at the bottom, according to Verol, or the whole thing would be useless. "For this," she said just as the door opened.

The two witches looked up to see Poem walk in with Verol and Amiri close behind. The two of them were bickering, though what about, Sella couldn't be sure. They fell silent as soon as they made it into the shop.

Verol stopped behind, but Amiri shoved her way forward. "Detective," she said with all the force of a storm crashing into the room. "This is unacceptable." She moved to stand between Sella and Poem with one hand out. "I will not allow this."

"Your authority ends where my jurisdiction begins," Poem said. He sidestepped her with ease. "Sella, I have enough reason and evidence to believe you are the one responsible for the death of Baziliari."

Sella sighed. She cut the tip of the mushroom carefully. "What evidence?" she said as she made a clean cut through. Her eyes flicked up.

"Excuse me?" Poem asked.

Verol peeked out from behind him. She bit her lip nervously.

"You said you have evidence. What evidence besides my use of fire?" She waited. He said nothing in return. "Because I don't think that is enough." Her words were strong, though her body felt weaker with each word.

"That's what I said." Verol nearly leapt ahead of Poem. "And he accused me of hiring you. With *no proof* by the way."

Although that would be poetic, Sella thought with a small snort escaping her. She was tired, but she was not afraid.

"The witches and the military have enough animosity," Amiri said. "Don't exasperate it."

"Or what?" Poem said.

Amiri's lips twitched. Then, she smiled. "Or we'll take you down, piece by piece. Together."

Verol pulled back, but she still pumped her fist behind Poem. A small, uncharacteristic gesture that had Sella raising a brow.

"Is that a threat?" Poem asked.

Sella raised her hands. She moved from behind the counter and approached the group with slow, steady steps. When she noticed that her shoulders were caving in, she straightened her posture quickly. She wasn't going to shrink. Not for him. Not for anyone. Not with so much at stake.

"I'll come with you to answer any questions you may have for me," she said. "But I didn't do this. Verol didn't do this. Amiri didn't do this. And I won't leave Sunfall with you."

"Alright," Poem said at last. "Come along then." He turned to the door as if completely unfazed by anything any of them had just said.

That felt too easy, Sella suspected she was walking into a trap.

Still, she nodded to Verol who stared at her with her eyes wide. She smiled back at Amiri and Sediri with what she hoped looked reassuring instead of nervousness. She wasn't anxious, though a part of her thought she really should be. Instead, she followed Poem out the door and into the bright sunlight with confident steps.

THE ROOM WAS WARMLY DECORATED. Not at all what Sella was expecting. Though, unless it was hidden somewhere, this town didn't have a jail or holding place. Sunfall must have been safe. Relatively, at least, before Baz died.

All around them were coarse textile rugs hanging from wood ladders in bold reds and yellows. The clay walls kept the inside cool though the light from the long narrow window shined brilliantly on the dark wood table, highlighting the swirling dust in the air between them.

Sella had been in this position before, though this time, it felt quite different. Back home, years ago, she sat across from a detective, not accused but in danger. She had lied then, and tried to keep herself and Lohrna safe. It hadn't gone well.

The position she had currently found herself in was certainly worse than it had been back then. And she had more people than just Lohrna to protect. But as she stared into Poem's eyes, quietly waiting for him to begin speaking, she could hear the steady beat of her heart in her chest and the deep and easy breathing through her nose.

She didn't have to wait long.

Poem folded his hands on the wooden table. "That was quite the spectacle in there," he said.

Sella smiled, though she didn't quite intend to. She pulled one side of her mouth back down into a thin line. "If you think so, you might have a rough time in Marra," she said honestly.

It was the truth. There, the small town was wild and loud and folks got into the occasional screaming fit when things got scary. By comparison, a low toned threat of comradery between longstanding opposing sides, was tame.

"How did you get the military on your side?" Poem asked as if reading her thoughts.

Sella shrugged. "It couldn't help that you blamed their leader," she said. "They seem loyal. Perhaps that was a miscalculation on your part."

Poem nodded. He raised his hands to his mouth and hummed.

"Why am I here other than my fire?"

Poem lowered his hands. "The barkeep had her property burned down by the wyvern rider. He comes back to town the first time since then, and he gets burned. It seems… convenient."

"I don't think so," Sella said. "No one in town knew they were coming. I have been here for a time before, helping Sediri set up her shop here while she traveled. I have a letter in my room from Kapilla. A kitchen witch coven back home. It asks me to come here to set up a competing shop."

"And will you?"

Sella's brows furrowed. "Of course not," she said. "You don't know me, detective, and you haven't cared to try. The military here is loyal to their own. I am to mine as well. But the letter is dated. It corroborates my story and my reasoning to be here."

"A forgery easy to create," he countered.

"And convoluted. If it was a fake, wouldn't I have a letter from Sediri herself asking me to come?"

Poem considered it. He leaned back in his chair. "Perhaps."

Sella stood, resting her hands on the table with the tips of her fingers. She felt warmth there, but called it back quickly. "You are going to do what you are going to do," she said. "But I urge you to consider all the evidence we have first. Because I won't leave this town with you." She turned to the door and thought she heard Poem say, "We'll see."

But she didn't have time to worry about him now. She

had to check on her friends. On Cali. She had to keep looking for the spell to help. She wasn't going home without it.

THIRTY-SEVEN

The Riders of Tollintal

"ARE YOU ALRIGHT?" Lohrna asked, grasping Sella's hands in her own as soon as Sella arrived back in the shop. She looked at the witch with a worried expression. "Verol told us you went with Poem? Why would you do that alone?"

"It's fine," Sella said. She squeezed Lohrna's hands and then released them gently. "It was just a talk."

Cali shimmered into view at Lohrna's side. "I'm sorry," she said. "I didn't know he'd escalate like that. I should have been there with you. Given him a scare." Her smile turned wicked and Sella laughed.

"No, I'm fine. Really," she told them both. "Poem thinks I'm to blame. Honestly, I'm surprised it took him this long to come for me." She looked around the shop, at Sediri busy behind the counter brewing something, at Verol and Lazil with their familiars at their sides. Each had a concern and unease etched into their faces. "Where's Amiri?" Sella asked the group.

Sediri looked up from her work. "She went to let the others know to prepare their wyverns."

"Prepare them?" Sella's own expression soured. "For what? Are they leaving?"

Sediri raised a brow. She slid a pot of herbal tea across the counter and the space filled with the scent of wet earth, musty and yet crisp with a hint of bright lemon. "They're going to show a display of strength, I suspect. At least they're on our side." She leaned forward and tapped on the pot. "Calming brew," Sediri said to the group. "Drink up."

"We're not going to let anyone take a witch," Verol said. "This town has had enough of outsiders coming in and messing with things."

Sella felt her chest tighten, though a calm smile fell on her lips. She was loved, protected. It was the first time in a very long time that she felt a sense of community. She had always been outside. Outside the folks in Marra. Outside the kitchen witches in Orakan. But here, she had a wand. She had her fire. And she was loved even if it didn't feel like home.

Lohrna squeezed her arm. "Sella, we still owe it to the town to find the killer," she said. "Don't we?"

Sella nodded.

Cali rested her head on Sella's shoulder gently. "Don't worry," she said. "Justice comes for everyone, eventually. We're smart, we'll figure it out."

Sella leaned into her touch and ease flowed through her. Her eyes moved about all the faces in the room. The witches who accepted her. Her best friend. The ghost she had fallen so deeply in love with.

Sediri poured the tea into mugs as a small scratch at the door interrupted their moment of calm.

Lohrna opened the door and Beejee squeezed through the small crack. "What ridiculous thing did we find ourselves in now?" he demanded. "Do they know they're talking to a powerful witch?"

Cali bent down to give him a little scratch along his back. "Oh, Beejee," she said. "I don't think anyone knows just how powerful you two truly are."

Sediri crossed the room and thrust a mug into Sella's hands. "Calm," she repeated. "I used your recipe."

Sella looked down into the steam. She breathed in the sweet smell of loam and clay. The hint of lemon tickled at the end. She drank it quickly. "Please tell me you gave some to Amiri before she left?"

Sediri nodded. "Though she was in a hurry, I'm not sure how much it will affect her in the state she was in."

"If it's our blend, it'll still work," Beejee said.

Sella could sense that Beejee desperately wanted to add a dig at Sediri. A jab about how their recipes were better than the weak ones she made back when she worked for Kapilla. Instead, he huffed and looked up at her. "What are we going to do about the rogue wyvern?"

"What do you mean?" Lazil asked with a cock of her head.

"Lucanairi," Sella explained. "Baz's wyvern. He's unbonded and unruly because of it. If they're bringing their wyverns into town, there's no telling what he'll do."

Lazil hummed. She crossed her arms and tapped herself lightly with her fingertips. "That could be a problem. If he thinks he needs to attack," she said. "But he can't use fire unless he uses *with* a rider, right?"

"That's true," Cali said. "He can still do a bit of damage, of course."

Lohrna jumped, throwing herself in the middle of the group. "I've got it!" she shouted. "I know what to do!"

THIRTY-EIGHT

Wyvern Pest Control

"Yes, yes, very dramatic," Beejee said after the stunned silence had gone on just a little too long. "What's the idea?"

Lohrna smiled ear to ear as she stood excitedly on her tiptoes, her black curls tangled in her thin antlers. "Lucanari. He's the only witness."

"Right, but they established it couldn't have been his —" Verol said slowly.

"Doesn't matter," Lohrna cut her off with her hands waving. "We've been so busy summoning ghosts and all that – no offence, Cal."

Cali held up her hands. "Not at all, ghosts are wonderful."

"But who we need to talk to is the wyvern," Lohrna went on. "We could give him the spell to talk, just like we did with Beejee and me, in my shifter form."

"Could that work?" Verol asked.

Sediri shrugged. "I don't see why it wouldn't?"

Cali rubbed her finger and thumb together, thoughtfully taking it all in. She grimaced a little and the witches all turned their attention to her.

Lohrna looked at the empty space where they all focused. "Oh no, what?" she asked.

Cali sighed. "It is possible, in theory," she said. "But I don't know if it would work in practice. Wyvern and their riders are deeply connected. They share their minds at times, in a way. From the stories I've heard, they don't really think the way we do. I don't know if they'd be able to communicate the way we do. The way a familiar does, the way Lohrna does. They think in images, emotions, something so far from what we do that I doubt we'd be able to understand, truly. At least, I doubt it'd be able to tell us who did it. If it did see at all, that is. I suspect if it knew who hurt Baz, Lucanairi would have gone after them himself."

Sella relayed the information to Lohrna and with each point, she watched her friend deflate lower and lower. She rubbed the back of Lohrna's shoulders. "It was a good idea, though," she reassured her.

"Yeah," Lohrna said with a heavy sigh. "Well, unless one of us bonds with the wyvern, then, I guess we're out of luck."

The group was silent for a long while. Each looked off into the ceiling or the floor, any place but each other.

Sella's mind raced despite the calm blend making its way into her system. She was grateful that Sediri had thought ahead. Though her mind was moving quickly, it was clear. Who could bond with a wyvern? Who would

Lucanairi even want? She took a long breath in and thought about their options.

"What does it take to bond with a wyvern?" Sella asked Cali at last.

Cali shrugged. "The wyvern has to pick you. Usually for a quality they hold in high regard."

Sella translated for Lohrna who made a small snort in return.

"Well, we don't have long to figure out what Lucanairi admires, then," Beejee said. "Ruthlessness?"

"Crulety?" Verol speculated with a small spit.

"Power?" Lazil's eyes lingered on Sella for a moment too long, making her uncomfortable. She didn't like the insinuation, though the better part of her knew the other witch meant nothing by it.

She was, indeed, powerful. Still, she shook her head. "Since he's been without Baz," she thought aloud, "Lucanairi has done what..?"

"Fly around being a menace," Beejee said. He jumped up onto the table to get a better vantage point. He looked at the familiar on Lazil's shoulder and grumbled back. "He slept on the hotel… Saved Cosas from the fire, but actually made it worse… Maybe he wants someone clumsy."

"He's eaten *a lot* of bugs," Cali added with a laugh.

Sella bit her lip gently. She tried to remember the wyvern's expressions when he was up on the roof. He had been stubborn, refusing to leave for anything but the command of Amiri and even then, he seemed to do it with an anger in his heart. A pain, perhaps, she saw that now and felt a sting her stomach rise into her throat. He had been hurting, perhaps in a way she could not imagine. And none of them had seen past his teeth and scales and claws to notice.

She remembered the way he snarled at her with his one wing covering Cosas. The protectiveness of his stance. What had the wyvern been doing on the roof? Could he have been guarding something?

"Tell us your thoughts," Lohrna said gently. She leaned down to catch Sella's eyes.

Sella smiled at her friend. "I know Baz could be a cruel man," she said. Her eyes moved to Verol. "I'm not saying he wasn't. But. I don't think that is what the wyvern values. I think it is the other side of security. Protectiveness." She shook her head, the words in her mind swirled and tumbled and she couldn't pick just one. "Lucanairi is a guardian at heart, I think Baz used that to his advantage."

Verol put one hand on her hip. "Perhaps," she said. "I don't like the idea of that, though."

Lazil shrugged. "Don't like it, but that doesn't mean it's not true. I think you might be on to something, Sella."

Sella's gaze focused on Lohrna at last. She raised an eyebrow.

"What?" Lohrna asked, pulling back from her. "You don't think... *Sella!*"

Sella shrugged. "I don't know," she said. "You're the most loyal and protective and kind hearted person I know. You'd do anything to help anyone in need, even run into fire."

Cali's smile widened. "Actually, you know what… that could work. Amiri would be furious to lose a wyvern, but it could work."

Lohrna looked at the space where Cali stood to Sella. "What'd she say? Did she say it's a terrible idea? Please tell me she said it won't work. What would I do with *a wyvern* in Marra?"

Sella laughed a little. "Doesn't Aadel need help keeping the pests out of your garden?"

Lohrna's brows rose. "Use Lucanairi for pest control?" she nearly shouted.

Verol put a firm hand on Lohrna's shoulder. "If this works, it could help us clear everyone's name in town. And bring the real killer to justice. Besides," she said with a warm smile. "Maybe Lucanairi deserves a quiet retirement by the sea. He's been through so much."

Lohrna groaned. "Getting to my heart, that's low," she said with a laugh. "Has a wylde ever even boded to a wyvern before?"

Outside, it sounded like a storm had blown in, though the light still poured through the window up front.

The wyverns were here. There was no more time to wonder or question.

Cali held Sella's hand. "She'll just need to ask," she said. "It's really stupidly simple."

THIRTY-NINE

The Bond

THE GROUP STEPPED out into the sunlight.

Sella held a hand up to shield her face as she blinked unsteadily, trying to see where the source of the wind that had just burst by came from.

She looked up.

Circling overhead the shapes of three wyverns dotted above, their silhouettes dark against the cloudless cerulean sky. She squinted at them.

Only three.

Where was Lucanairi?

She turned to Lohrna, but she was already pointing down the road to Poem who was fast approaching.

"What is the meaning of this?" he asked when we grew close. He looked up at the sky, following their gazes. "Where is the fourth?"

"That's what we're wondering," Beejee said.

Sella turned to Poem, though her hand remained over her face. "We have a plan," she said quickly. "I'm not saying it will work, but it just might be the only way to solve this."

Poem narrowed his eyes. But then he glanced up at the wyverns again. "Alright, I'm listening."

Sella recounted their idea as sparsely as she could. She grabbed onto Lohrna's hand. "All she has to do is ask," she said. "It's worth a try."

Poem's chin lifted. "Perhaps," he said.

Suddenly, the first wyvern darted down, followed by the other two close behind. They dove down to the left, toward the open square.

"Come on," Lazil said with a strange smile. "Let's go meet them."

"Why do you look so chipper?" Sella heard Verol grumble under her breath.

But she didn't have time to linger. The group rushed down the road and toward the square.

It was empty of its usual booths and people. But the wide space was full as the three wyverns stretched out their wings, standing tall on their long legs.

A small gathering of townsfolk had joined them there, everyone looking up at the wyverns and their riders with suspicion and fear. Sella watched Cosas in the back, he was holding a pan close to his chest as though it would save him from whatever was coming next. Beside him, a group of older women huddled together, glaring at the creatures with grimaces on their lips.

From behind the three, Lucanairi appeared between the shadows of the buildings. His ability to hide himself among the structures was something Sella could never quite get used to. She stopped in her tracks.

Amiri spoke, her voice booming from atop the wyvern, "We do not intend to let your power here go unchecked."

"We have a plan," Poem said boldly from the back of their little group.

Sella scoffed. But she kept her posture straight and did not turn to him. If he wanted to take credit, he may as well. She approached Amiri's wyvern with careful steps. "Cali helped," she said softly. "Trust us." Then, louder, she said, "Lohrna might be able to see the truth of the matter. If she can bond with Lucanairi."

Amiri's mouth fell open. She turned to the other two behind her.

Tate merely shrugged.

Motet turned to the lone wyvern. He looked back at Sella, then to Amiri. "It may be the only way," he said.

Amiri sat taller on her own wyvern. Beneath her, it shifted on its two strong legs, flapped its powerful wings once, then settled. She looked at Lohrna with a stern expression. "Try," she said.

Sella wasn't sure it was a challenge or a threat. But Lohrna didn't seem to care. For all her protests before, she stepped toward the creatures with confidence in her stride.

Amiri called to Lucanairi in a language Sella didn't recognize. All she knew was that it was a command, meaning 'Come here' because, with his head lowered and long neck slinking forward, Lucanairi approached the center of the square.

Lohrna smiled at him as she took a deep breath. She held out her hands carefully, slowly. "Hi, friend," she said gently. "I don't know if you can understand all of this, or... any of this. But I'm trying to find justice for your previous rider. And... I'm asking you to... bond with me to help with this."

Lucanairi growled low. His head swayed as he looked at Lohnra with each large reptilian eye.

She lowered her hands, but didn't back away. "If we're bonded, that means we have to be together, I think," she whispered, so low that Sella almost didn't hear. "We would go back to Marra together. It's cold there, lots of rain. But you'd live a peaceful life. No wars. No battles. No traveling to enforce anything." She took one step closer. "You could protect our crops from pixies," she added with a light laugh. "They come out every new moon. Oh, and I should be clear... I turn into a really big wolf on the full moon. I understand if that's a deal-breaker."

Lucanairi snorted, the puff of air blew some of Lohrna's curls from her face. His neck extended and Lohrna closed her eyes.

Sella's heart beat loudly in her chest now. Anxiety spiked in her stomach, radiating out into her limbs until they all felt cold as ice. She held her wand in her pocket tight with frigid fingers.

Lohrna gasped and Sella drew her wand.

"Wait!" Lohrna cried, holding her arm up to stop Sella's magic. "I see…" she said. "I see…"

Sella turned to Cali at her side.

"She's done it!" Cali said with a clap. "We're bringing a wyvern home!"

Lucanairi pushed up on Lohrna's shoulder with his massive head. She stumbled back but held onto his snout with both arms. "Whoa there," she said with a little chuckle. "I'm not a big soldier."

Lucanairi pulled back, snorted again, then tossed his head to Sella.

Lohrna's laugh grew louder. "Yeah, she's your first choice. She already has a familiar."

Sella's eyebrow twitched up. Lohrna sounded like she was joking with it.

"Can you see what happened to Baziliari?" Poem asked, stepping forward.

Lohrna nodded. "Let me try…" She sat down in the square as all around, the townsfolk began to speak, some loudly, some in harsh whispers. She didn't seem to care. She simply closed her eyes and Lucanairi moved to curl his wing around her, shading her from the sunlight and the noise. A small smile fell on her lips, and then, she was hidden in his wing.

A moment passed, then another. The noise around them grew louder and louder, until, at last, Lucanairi's wing lifted and Lohrna rose from her seat. She patted the wyvern's snout with one hand. "Go fly, you've earned it. As far as you want," she whispered. Then, to the detective, the witches, and the soldiers, she said louder, "That was the strangest thing I've ever experienced. Let's go somewhere… private to talk. Please?"

IN THE EMPTY TAVERN, most of the group sat at the bar, each with their own drink in hand.

Lohrna and Verol stood on the other side. Verol, leaning up against the wood with one hip and Lohrna clutching her own mug with both hands.

"Cali is right," Lohrna said at last. "I saw images more than words. And feelings. Poor Lucanairi…" She sipped the wine from her cup slowly, then looked up at them. "I can't explain how it happened. But Baz died by his own wyvern fire."

"I knew it," Poem said. "Easy to deduce, really."

Each witch turned to him slowly, anger flaring in their eyes.

From behind him, Cali pinched the back of his neck.

He flinched, turning half way as he smacked the back of his neck.

Cali winked at Sella. "What? He's ridiculous."

Lohrna sighed and took another slow sip. "They were in the forge," she explained. "Lucanairi and Baz and Motet. They were arguing about something. Something they both felt strongly about. But Luca didn't understand what." She turned to Motet, waiting.

Amiri nodded to him. "Now's the time to tell it how it was, soldier. They should know."

Motet let out a heavy breath. He looked down at his drink and Tate squeezed his shoulder, prompting him to speak. Instead, Motet tilted his drink back and grimaced at the burn in his throat. He shook his head, hanging it low.

He spoke, his voice a low whisper, "Baziliari wanted us to break command. Extort the town and the witches here. I told him I wouldn't. That I'd report him to Amiri if he gave the order to burn anything here. That was the last thing I ever said to him."

Lohrna nodded, though lines between her brows deepened. She took his hand from across the bar and held it carefully. "Luca showed me that you left after that and just when you were out of sight… Baz ordered Lucanairi to fire, but… Luca didn't understand why. He blew fire, but when Baz went to direct it, it backfired somehow. He was gone in a flash. Just like that. He didn't suffer."

The group sat in stunned silence. Hardly anyone breathed as they let the story settle like dust between them.

"Baziliari meant to murder me?" Motet said at last, his voice was low, disbelief heavy in his tone. "I never would have thought…"

"Well," Lohrna said, "Lucanairi doesn't see it that way. But, objectively, yes. You got lucky."

"Sounds like we all did," Cali breathed.

"When are we ever lucky?" Beejee said from his seat beside Sella.

Sella's eyes lowered to him. She smiled. He was right. They had gotten lucky… At every turn. They had gotten lucky. The realization hit her like a wave. She choked as if spitting up water. "Lucky!"

Everyone turned to her but she was too busy leaping from her chair to notice. "Motet, you tried the special. Our lucky blend!"

His eyes shifted down, as if he was about to argue that nothing lucky had happened to him when his eyes widened suddenly.

"We thought it didn't work," Sella explained to Sediri, her smile growing. "But it did! Just… It worked *too well*. It was meant for things like finding a coin on the ground, or guessing the right route to work… but. The fire meant for you, Motet, it backfired onto Baz! And think about us." She turned to Lohrna, then Beejee. "We just happened to make the wrong thing, but then we got the right ingredients for something else. We just happened to find the right books we needed at the right times. We're lucky! Unbelievably, life-alteringly lucky!"

"Of course," Poem said. "It all makes perfect sense."

Verol raised a brow. "Does it?"

"It does if you're lucky," Poem said as he tapped his temple.

The Rain

SELLA BREWED herself and the witches one last batch of the speciality brew.

Sediri was certain that she could keep the recipe as it was, that if *she* made it, it would be back to what it was meant to be: an extra opportunity for little moments of luck throughout the day.

As Sella held her hands around the large pot, she set her intention. Luck finding the perfect spell for Cali. She opened one eye at the group all gathered at the table. "Can we raid your bookstore after?" Sella asked. "There's one more spell I need before we leave."

"Of course," Lazil said. "You're my friend. You're welcome to anything I have." On her shoulder, her familiar made a chirping sound.

Sella smiled. "Thank you," she said as she crossed the space with her speciality blend in hand. Notes of chestnut and cinnamon filled the air. Just a hint of spice, and a tang of bitter grounds followed her. Everyone at the table perked up, their noses in the air. She poured each witch her own cup, then sat down among them.

While she had longed to be home and back to all she knew and loved, there was a part of her that knew she'd miss this, too. She almost wished they had more time together.

Almost.

Sella the fire starter. Sella the wand breaker. Sella and *The Incidents.*

None of those defined her here. She was just a witch. Sitting among other witches.

She drank her brew slowly as rain began to tap lightly on the window. She knew by now that this was temporary. That the rain would come sidewise soon enough, and thunder would crack open the sky. But that was temporary too. By twilight, the sky would turn golden and red and pink. The intense pigments would fade out into the darkness, the sky would turn black, and she'd be submerged in a sea of stars and then, the morning sun would rise.

She looked to the window, half listening to the conversation the witches were having about the future of their town after all this, and half wondering if Lohrna and the soldiers were alright in the barn, feeding wyverns bugs. But most of her wondered how Cali was feeling. What she was doing now.

SELLA HAD little evidence to prove it, but she felt certain in her heart that it was best to go looking for what she sought as soon as possible. The lucky brew seemed to have a lingering effect, but she couldn't take the risk.

As she opened the door to the potion shop, the wind and rain hit her hard in the face, however, she felt that braving the storm was a risk on its own.

"It's locked but unwarded!" Lazil called from the safety of the indoors. "Just let yourself in!"

Sella simply nodded and, with Beejee dauntlessly at her side, they ventured out into the storm.

SELLA FLICKED her wrist and the door to the narrow bookshop opened. She and Beejee pushed inside quickly and she ignited a series of fires overhead to light their way. At her feet, Beejee shook off water all over the floor.

"Careful of the books," Sella said, though she was dripping water onto the floor as well. Still, she didn't shake out her hair or her clothes as much as she desperately wanted to.

The wind outside and the tap tap tap of the water hitting the wooden floor at her feet sounded like a song she had long ago forgotten. It played at the edges of her mind as the fires floated back toward her, lighting the rows and stacks of books among them.

Sella looked down at Beejee, who was staring intently at one of the books on top of a stack on the floor. It was covered in rainwater, slowly soaking through to the pages.

He looked up at her. "Do you think she'll notice?"

Sella grumbled a little. She lit a small fire in the palm of her hand and picked up the book carefully as water spilled to the floor, beading off the cover with ease. "It looks to be undamaged," she said.

"Good," Beejee said as he trotted off to examine other piles. "We can't afford to replace it."

Sella turned the old book over in her hands. "I don't think most of these *are* replaceable," she whispered. This book was old. The edges of the pages were worn a dark tan, and the binding was coming loose, the stitching hanging on, though clearly in desperate need of repair. She flipped it back over to look closer at the cover. "A Comprehensive Guide to Spellwork for the Dead Beside Us," she whispered the title aloud.

Beejee turned back to her. His ear flicked. "Don't tell me it could have been this easy the whole time," he said.

Sella opened the book, flipping to a random page, then another, then another. She looked up at Beejee. "We're lucky, but not that lucky," she said. "All these spells need something more powerful than me. A Niminé."

Beejee let out a little sigh. "Even when we're lucky, there's a loose knot."

FORTY-ONE

What It Means to Live

THE KNOCK on the door was so quiet that Sella almost didn't hear it. Beejee was curled up on the corner of the bed in their little hotel room. His tail flicked. "Are you going to get that?" he asked.

The knock came again, this time, a little stronger.

Sella let out a small groan as she rose from the bed. It was late and she was tired. On unsteady feet, she crossed the room quietly, trying to not wake Lohrna, though she miscalculated along the way and she heard the floorboards creak with every step. She grimaced, opening the door which also protested on squeaky hinges.

Lohrna rolled over and let out a heavy sigh. "Whaaaat?"

So much for luck.

In the doorway, Amiri stood with her hands behind her back and a weary gaze fixed to the floor.

Sella felt a jolt burst through her, waking her instantly.

"Amiri–" she started, straightening her dress as best she could.

Amiri held a hand out to quiet her. "I understand the hour is late," she said, a strange formality in her words.

Sella looked her up and down, at her posture, her stance, the way she held her hands loose behind her. Sella hadn't been around the soldiers much. But she did notice that when they were with a higher rank, their whole demeanor changed like this. As though they were operating by a set of rules she was not cognizant of. Something had happened.

"You're leaving?" Sella asked.

Amiri nodded. Her eyes finally made their way to Sella where they softened and a small, tired smile fell on her lips. "I want to speak to Calisyali one more time," she said. "If I can."

Cali appeared behind Sella, sending a shiver up her back. "Let's go to her room," she said. "I don't want to wake Lohrna."

Sella turned over her shoulder, trying to silently ask 'Are you sure?'

Cali nodded, her smile reached her eyes. "Grab the sheet," she said.

Sella looked back at Amiri. "We'll be in your room in a moment," she said as she began to close the door gently.

Just before it clicked shut, she heard Amiri's quiet whisper, "Thank you."

• • •

AMIRI'S ROOM WAS SMALL. A little bed was pushed up against the wall, and even still, a two seat table barely fit.

The soldier sat across from the ghost, a plain sheet over her head and a set of glasses perched over her nose which created enough crease in the sheet that Sella could almost tell Cali's profile.

Sella sat on the bed, her feet pulled up to her chest and her head resting on her knees.

"I'll just say what she says," Sella said quietly. "I'll say it exactly."

Amiri looked at Sella, then to Cali. She took in a shuddering breath before her eyes flicked up to the ceiling, trying to hold back tears. One fell from her eye regardless and she pushed it off her cheek with the back of her hand. "I'm sorry," she said at last. She pushed her shoulders back and looked at Cali with the old authority and confidence back on her face. "I shouldn't be crying when you're the one who's gone."

"But I'm not gone," Cali said, with Sella soon after. "I'm right here."

"It's not the same," Amiri said.

Cali laughed, the sheet ruffled a little as her shoulders shook with the force. "I was gone before. Why is this different?"

Sella translated, and added at the end, "Cali's laughing."

Amiri's lips pulled into a thin line. "It's definitive now," she said.

Cali shrugged. "Nothing is really *definitive*. You're closer to me now than you have been in years."

Amiri shook her head. "How can you be so…"

"I'm happy," Cali cut her off and Sella followed. "I wish things were different sometimes, but I'm happy. I get to haunt, which is fun. I have Lohnra, and Beejee. My own cat back home in Marra. I have Sella." Cali's form turned to Sella on the bed and the witch knew, beneath the sheet, she was smiling.

Though pain ripped into her heart, Sella knew, just as Amiri wondered, that it sometimes felt impossible for Cali was truly happy as she was. It was a strange thing. But they weren't Cali, and they didn't have the right to tell her how to feel.

Cali went on, leaning forward a little, "Though Sella didn't notice me until I was dead. Which I think is wild. We make an excellent couple."

Sella paused.

Cali turned to her. "You have to say all of it," she scolded.

Sella paraphrased. She still felt guilty whenever Cali reminded her that Sella had never noticed her flirtations in life. Even stranger to now admit to her sister that they had fallen in love only after death.

"Will you tell the family?" Cali asked quickly.

"Do you want me to?" Amiri questioned her with a raised brow.

Cali shook her head. "No need. I like having a secret with you."

Amiri breathed deeply. She smiled, but her eyes still shimmered with tears. "I miss you," she whispered. "I missed you before you died, and I miss you now."

"Come visit Marra sometime," Cali said. "You can say you're checking in on Lucanairi so the higher ups will let you go."

Amiri nodded. But she didn't speak.

Cali moved forward again. "You can be with me whenever you want to," she said quietly. "Whenever you make a choice to do something silly, or try to talk instead of fight… or do some math…" Cali added the last part with a giggle. "You'll be with me."

Amiri folded in. Her elbows hit the table and she covered her face with her hands. Tears spilled from her eyes and she sucked in a quivering breath. "Cali–"

"Oh stop that," Cali said with a lightness in her tone. She sounded kind and bright but Sella couldn't bring herself to tell Amiri to hold back her cries. "It happens to us all. One day, you'll be here too."

Sella spoke Cali's words and watched Amiri's breathing grow deeper. She kept her face hidden, though, eventually, her tears subsided. She looked small. Almost delicate. So unlike any perception Sella had held about her before. It felt wrong to sit here watching this. And yet, all she wanted to do was reach out and hold them both. To say she was sorry, though she wasn't sure for what.

"I was happy then, and I'm happy now," Cali said at last. "Just… live. In a way that makes you happy."

Amiri sniffed. She pushed herself up and set her shoulders again. Her nose and the rims of her eyes were red in the flickering candlelight. "I'll try," she said.

Cali laughed. "That's all any of us can do."

· · ·

THE SOLDIERS DID NOT GET the farewell that Sella anticipated. No one came into the square to wish them well, or yell for them to get out of there and never return. In fact, no one but Sella and Cali were there at all.

It was almost disappointing to watch the wyverns take off into the sky in silence, leaving behind a town they had both broken and repaired, though Sella suspected it would never be quite the same as it once was. Perhaps, that was a good thing.

Sella watched as their forms became smaller and smaller, until at last, they disappeared from sight. She waited for a few moments, unsure of what to say or if she should be saying anything at all.

Cali's hand, solid for now, found Sella's. "Have we given any thought to how we're going to transport Lucanairi?"

Sella laughed, and suddenly, the weight of everything lifted from her mind. She looked down at Cali. "You know, the only way might be to fly," she said.

"Beejee will kill you," Cali said as she nudged her with her shoulder. She passed right through.

"Then I'd be with you," Sella said simply. She looked back up at the sky. "What's the first thing you'll do when you can talk to anyone?"

Cali hummed. "Probably tell Hazen his bookkeeping is still atrocious."

Sella snorted.

"What? It is. I go in there at night sometimes to see if he's keeping the organizational systems I set up and he hasn't at all. All that hard work, and for what?"

Sella squeezed Cali's hand gently. "I'm sure he'll be thrilled to hear your voice, even if you're scolding him."

Cali shimmered out of sight, her hand passed through Sella's fingers like smoke. "Go see the witches of Sunfall," she said. "I've had enough goodbyes for now."

SELLA, Lohrna, and Beejee stood outside the potion shop, none of them quite ready to open the door.

Their trip had been shorter than they expected. And yet, more eventful, horrifying, and fulfilling than they could have ever anticipated. Sella tried to recount all they had done, all they had experienced here, and still, it felt like too much to contain in one memory. She suspected that it would take a long while at home to feel like all this wasn't some strange dream.

Nevertheless, as Sediri opened the door and stared at them with a slight scowl, Sella knew that she'd carry these unexpected friendships in her heart, even if she couldn't recall how they had gotten there.

"Well, come in," Sediri said. "Verol and Lazil are waiting for you."

Lohrna bounded into the shop, with Beejee close behind. Sella followed, though her feet moved slower. She wasn't sure she was ready for goodbyes yet either, but as she entered the cozy shop, she felt, at long last, a feeling of lightness wash over her.

Lohrna was already talking about flying the wyvern back home, excitedly waving her arms around as the witches listened in captivated silence. "And now Sella won't be the only fire user in Marra!" she added at the end.

"I'm sure no one will let us forget *The Incident* though," Beejee said with a huff.

Sella shrugged as she approached the group. "I don't know, a giant creature might at least keep people from asking *us* too many questions," she said with a smile.

Beejee blinked at her slowly.

Lazil leaned on the counter. "What 'incident'?" she asked.

Sella waved her hand. "No time," she deflected the question. "We wanted to say thank you." She looked at each witch and wanted so desperately to tell them every reason she had to be grateful to know them. For the community. For the wand. For trusting her enough to let her find her power. For the spell to help Cali. But all she said was, "Thank you. For... everything."

Verol crossed the space between them and with gentle arms, she pulled Sella and Lohran close to her. She smelled of earth and rain and cinnamon.

Sella breathed in deeply and felt her body settle into the witch's embrace. Lohrna was warm, and Verol's hold on them was strong. They both squeezed a little tighter and in that moment, Sella was at peace.

FORTY-TWO

Welcome Back, Cali

It was a rainy afternoon in Marra, though inside her mother's old house, sunlight shone through stained glass windows, casting colorful dots along the wood floor.

The spell was one Sella had never been able to perform but she also wasn't so sure she ever wanted to. She liked the rain and felt a strange contentment knowing that this particular spell was only cast here. A clean, warm house where the sun was always bright.

Sella sat across from Seaglass, steam from their mugs creating a wall of spiraling silver between them. For the first time since their return to Marra years ago, Beejee had entered the house. He sat beside Sella on the table, staring at Seaglass with narrowed eyes.

The fact that a Niminé had been tending to her mother's house had been a shock when Sella first discovered their presence. The first time they met, Sella expected the house to be empty and unkept from sitting empty. Instead, she found Seaglass coming out from the kitchen, already brewing up a batch of tea for them both.

The legendary sea creature was child-sized, though that did nothing to prevent the twinge of fear that Sella still felt in their presence especially since their large, silver, and pupilless eyes seemed to always be staring right through her, to the core of who she was.

Seaglass was deadly looking, despite their small stature. Thin, spider-like limbs moved with grace and swiftness whenever they reached for something and long, sharp nails clinked along the mug when they grew impatient with Sella's agitation. It all reminded Sella that this creature was old and swift and sharp.

Now, as Seaglass smiled at Sella, several rows of shark teeth gnashed.

How, or why, the creature had risen from the depths of the ocean and come to land was still unknown to her. As was the way it met her mother and why it decided to honor the promise to look after the place when she was gone.

Still, the ancient spells required the magic of a Niminé, so Sella had to assume that once, long ago, witches and Niminé must have cooperated.

At least some of the time.

Sella said nothing. Instead, she brought the mug to her lips and sipped carefully. She savored the familiar smell of fallen leaves and rich wet dirt, the finish of lavender lingering on her tongue as she swallowed.

"I can perform the spell," Seaglass said at last as their smile faded. "But a spell like this…"

Sella waited. Her heart began to thud loudly. She was so close… She had come so far to help Cali, exhausted every option known to her. "I'll do anything," she said when she could no longer contain her words.

"But will your ghost?" Seaglass said with a cock of their head. "To cast this spell would mean that Calisyali will not be in our world, or the world of those who have gone before us. It is a cruel fate for any spirit. I will not cast this as written."

Sella lurched forward, her stomach grew sick as if she had just been hit.

Sealgass waved a long fingered hand. "Quiet yourself. I can modify the spell." Seaglass moved their head a little, turning toward the door. "You won't have a body. Not really. And I will need to tie your spirit to something living so you can be free. Eventually."

Cali shimmered into existence by the front door. She smiled brightly and Sella sighed, her heart heavy with relief. She had no idea that Cali would be here, but she was glad to see her.

"So I would need to tie my heart to something living. And when that person dies, I will be gone from here, too?" Cali asked.

"It is the only way to avoid you becoming trapped here, fitting into no world," Seaglass said with a small nod.

Cali tools a few steps closer, seemingly unafraid or even hesitant about the Niminé at all. She was still smiling, her expression warm. "And this modified spell… people will be able to see me and hear me?"

"The same way the witches can," Seaglass said. "You will be pulled closer to the world of the living. But it won't be complete."

"I'll do it, then," Cali said with a quick nod. She looked at Sella, crinkles forming at the corners of her eyes.

"I will too," Beejee said.

Seaglass and Sella turned to him quickly.

The familiar looked up at the ceiling as if he hadn't said anything at all. "What?" he said at last. "Tie yourself to me. I'm safe and will live for a long time, if we're lucky."

Cali's hands clasped over her heart. "Beejee!"

"But you owe me," he said, the corner of his mouth twitched into a silly little smile.

LOHRNA PACED OUTSIDE the house with an uncharacteristic agitation in her movement. They found her among the beehives, worrying at the fabric of her skirt.

"Everything alright?" Cali asked as she, Sella, and Beejee approached. "Lucanairi didn't do anything, did he?"

Lohrna looked up, eyes wide. Her hands fell to her side, then flew to her mouth. "Cal!" she cried, tearing through the lavender flowers to get to her. "It worked!" She threw her arms around the ghost, only to pass right through. "Oh…" she said with a laugh, "still a ghost. Right."

Cali's smile widened. She rested her head on Sella's shoulder. "Still a ghost," she said. "Beejee and I are bonded now."

Lohrna cast a look down at the little gray tabby cat.

He looked proud of himself, tail high in the air, chin up. "And I intend to live forever," he joked.

Sella's head tilted down to rest on top of Cali's. She was as solid as ever and a rush of relief filled Sella's body. Her limbs tingled with excitement, her chest light. After everything, rushing from place to place to find the spell, after first being reluctant to even help her at all, after fumble after fumble, Cali was finally here.

As here as she could be.

"Let's go see everyone," Sella said.

Cali nearly jumped, her expression more joyous than Sella had seen in a long time. She took Sella's hand. "And then, tea at home, please!"

"Of course," Sella said.

Lohrna led the way down the path toward town. "And scones!"

Sella smiled. She squeezed Cali's hand and they followed.

"And scones," Sella confirmed.

The group left the rhythmic sounds of the waves and buzzing bees behind, knowing that the house by the shore would be there when they needed it. That Seaglass would see Sella coming and prepare a blend of tea that wasn't quite right but still reminded her of home.

They were back at last, on their way to familiar faces, friendly voices, and old cobblestone streets that they knew every part of. Back to the seaside town that was merely a speck on the map.

They were home.

But as Sella watched Lohrna journey ahead, with Beejee at her side, heard them speak excitedly to each other about the sea monster and Lucanairi and what Hazen would say when he saw Cali, a warmth spread through her and she knew that home was wherever they were.

Cali swung Sella's arm, the movement shaking her from the depth of her thoughts and back to the moment, the feeling of Cali's happiness beside her and the crisp chill in the air just as a sprinkle of rain began to fall.

The End...

For now.

They're busy perfecting potions, staying up too late, and stumbling into more mysteries.

See you soon back home.

Tollintal Ice Coffee

Ingredients

- Your Favorite Coffee
- Ice
- Cinnamon
- Creamer (any kind)

Directions

1. Add cinnamon to the coffee grounds prior to brewing
2. Brew Your Favorite Coffee x 2 stronger than usual
3. Be patient. Let the coffee cool in fridge.
4. Fill a cup with ice and pour cooled coffee
5. Top with a splash of creamer

Notes

To make this magical, set an intention for the brew as you sprinkle cinnamon.
When waiting for the coffee to cool, practice gratitude for the earth, the workers, and the journey that got these beans to you

Sediri's Chill Out Blend

Ingredients

- Your Favorite Coffee
- Honey (1 - 2 tsp)
- Orange Peel
- Creamer (any kind)

Directions

1. Brew your coffee
2. Add honey to taste (start small, you can always add more)
3. Add a splash of creamer
4. Stir well until honey is melted through
5. Top with a twist of orange peel on top

Notes

To make this magical, set an intention for the day as you twist the orange peel
Take a moment to savor the citrus aroma

Sella's
Good Morning , Good Luck
Scones

Ingredients

- 2 cups all purpose flour
- ⅓ cup granulated sugar
- 2 teaspoon baking powder
- ½ teaspoon baking soda
- ¼ teaspoon salt
- 1/2 teaspoon ground cinnamon
- ⅛ teaspoon ground allspice
- ¼ cup chilled unsalted butter
- 1 cup peeled & cubed Honeycrisp apples
- ⅔ cup buttermilk
- 1 large egg
- 1 teaspoon vanilla extract
- Sprinkle of luck

Directions

1. Preheat oven to 400 ºF. Line baking sheet with parchment paper.
2. In a bowl, whisk flour, granulated sugar, baking powder, baking soda, salt, cinnamon, & allspice.
3. Dice butter into 1/2" cubes and cut the butter into the flour mixture.
4. Fold in the apples.
5. Whisk together buttermilk, egg, and vanilla extract.
6. Make a dent in the center of the flour and apple mixture and pour in the buttermilk mixture.
7. Use a spoon, and mix until just combined.
8. Pour the mixture onto a floured surface and press out into an 8" circle.
9. Use a knife to cut the dough into wedges and place them on the prepared baking sheets.
10. Bake for 18-22 minutes, or until slightly golden brown.
11. Let cool on a baking sheet for 5 minutes before transferring them to a wire cooling rack to cool completely.
12. Enjoy!

Notes

There are no notes. Good luck!

Acknowledgments

First, I would like to thank coffee.

That may very well be because it is 4am right now and I am watching my coffee machine brew me a pot at the moment, but do want to take the moment to recognize that I am lucky to have this pot of coffee.

I'm thankful to the farmers, the roasters, the workers who got it here, and the staff of my local Trader Joes. All of whom made this book possible.

This book was a little shorter than the others, but hopefully just as deeply rich for you. It is in the little things, the small moments, like having coffee now, where the magic of life happens. Okay, I'll stop wax poetically about coffee now. I just think it's important to stop sometimes and be thankful for and realize how much work goes into little things like this.

I'd like to thank my friends and family who have not given up on me throughout this process, even when sometimes I don't have much energy as deadlines loom, and especially when I have given up on myself– even if that only lasts a moment or two.

This journey is difficult and without my loved ones checking in on me, believing in me, and supporting me, I would be fueled solely by spite. And while that is a good motivator, I find it is best used as a last resort rather than sustained energy.

So, thank you to everyone who also said, "Well, you gave it a shot." Because when I'm too sad for loving words to find me, these ones do.

Thank you to my daughter who points to my books in stores and gets excited when I tell her I need to go do some writing.

Thank you to my son for spilling your food everywhere. It reminds me to let go of the little things and that deadlines aren't as important as the life that happens in between.

And thank you to my spouse for taking over the nightshift with the little guy so this book could happen.

Thank you to John for always checking that the next book is coming out.

Thank you to Shammy for driving far to meet me at a book signing that no one else showed up to. I will never forget it and it was truly the only thing that stopped me from breaking down in tears and questioning my life choices. Okay, I questioned them a little. But I didn't cry and that's because of your amazing friendship.

Thank you to Paige for encouraging me. Our nights tougher talking about everything from this book to just being are ones I treasure.

To Amphi for the chaos in which we both thrive. Without your guidance, how else would I be able to communicate with other artists? My anxiety would be too great and I would simply expire.

To you-know-who-you-both-are if you made it this far because without you, I'd still be in the dreaming phase.

Thank you to Sammy for supporting me every single time. I honestly don't know how you are so kind and wonderful but I hope you always know that you are.

To all my friends who read my books and those who don't.

Thank you readers who have become my true friends. And the ones who think my writing stinks, too. We need you all in the world.

Thank you again, coffee. I do wish I was a kitchen witch so I could add a little more self-compassion to my blend. But for now, this cup will have to do.

About the Author

Wren Jones lives in the Sonoran Desert with her family and two cats. Like most writers, she has been a storyteller for a long time. She is known for doing "the most" at the oddest times. Like deciding to pursue a writing career (finally) while raising two humans and working full time in a public school. She writes what she'd want to read: Stories where things turn out alright in the end.